King of Beasts

(BEAST DUET, BOOK 1)

DIANA A. HICKS

HMG, INC.

Copyright

King of Beasts, Beast Duet Book 1

Publishing History

Print ISBN 978-1-949760-32-3

Digital ISBN 978-1-949760-31-6

Credits

Cover Model: Christoph

Photographer: Wander Aguiar Photography

Cover Designer: Veronica Larsen

Editor: Tera Cuskaden and Becky Barney

Recommended Reading Order

The Crime Society World

Beast Duet

Lost Raven - Novella

King of Beasts (Beast Duet #1)

King of Beasts (Beast Duet #2)

Wolf Duet

Wolf's Lair - Prequel

Big Bad Wolf (Wolf Duet #1)

Big Bad Wolf (Wolf Duet #2)

Once Upon A Christmas - Bonus Epilogue

Raven Duet

Dark Beauty - Prequel

Fallen Raven (Raven Duet, #1)

Fallen Raven (Raven Duet, #2)

Knight Duet

Wicked Knight (Knight Duet, #1)

Wicked Knight (Knight Duet, #2)

Cole Brothers World

Stolen Hearts Duet

Entangle You

Unravel You

Steal My Heart Series

Ignite You

Escape You

Escape My Love - Bonus Epilogue

Provoke You

Cole Twins Duet

Unleash You

Defy You

Praise for Diana A. Hicks

"Hicks' first installment of her Desert Monsoon series is confident and assured with strong storytelling, nuanced characters, and a dynamic blend of romance and suspense."

— **KIRKUS REVIEWS**

What makes any romance a great read isn't the fact that two hot people meet and fall in love. It is the episodes that bring about the falling in love and the unexpected places the experience takes the characters that make it an enjoyable read. Diana A. Hicks knows just how to make this happen.

— **READERS' FAVORITE**

About the Author

Diana A. Hicks is an award-winning author of dark mafia romance and steamy contemporary romance with a heavy dose of suspense.

When Diana is not writing, she enjoys kickboxing, hot yoga, traveling, and indulging in the simple joys of life like wine and chocolate. She lives in Atlanta and loves spending time with her two children and husband.

Check out my bookstore!

Don't forget to sign up to my newsletter to stay up to date on my latest releases, free content, and other news.
Subscribe to my VIP List now!

SINFULLY DARK ROMANCE

Dear Readers,

I'm so happy to share Rex and Caterina's epic love story with you!

King of Beasts is a dark mafia romance that blends in elements of one of my favorite fairytales, Beauty and the Beast and kink.

This book has been on my mind for over a year, and I'm so happy that I finally get to share it with you!!! You're going to love Rex and Caterina's intense love story.

Don't forget to download the totally free bonus novella, featuring Massimo, Caterina's brother.

Lost Raven - Novella (FREE)

Get ready to fall in love with the ruthless men of the Society.

Welcome to The Society!

Diana

CHAPTER 1
Do You Have an Invitation?

CATERINA

"Five more minutes." I hit the screen on my phone to snooze the blaring alarm.

When nothing happened, I opened one eye to make sure I tapped the right button this time. Then I saw Dad's serene face on the incoming call. I scrambled to sit up and quickly pressed the device to my ear.

"Hello? Dad?"

"Caterina, it's me."

"I know, Dad. What's wrong?" I squinted at my watch. "It's one in the morning."

"I know. I'm sorry to wake you, Bells. I need a lift." He puffed out a breath. "You said last week, I could call any time."

My entire body sunk deeper into the mattress. *"I need a lift,"* was code for *"I spent all my money gambling and now I don't even have money for a cab."* Dad's addiction was getting worse.

1

"Text me your address. I'll come get you."

"I'm at the Crucible."

I stopped midway with my mouth open and feet hovering over the hardwood floor. *Fuck me.* Why that place? "Okay. I'll, um, I'll be there shortly."

"Thank you. You're the best daughter an old man like me could ask for."

"I'm on my way."

"I am so sorry to do this to you, Bells. You have no idea." His breath rustled on the speaker.

"See you soon, Dad." I tapped on the screen.

These middle-of-the-night calls were getting out of hand. I had a job to go to. I couldn't sit here and listen to Dad drone on about Mom. I was hurting too. A pang of remorse washed over me. I was all the family the old man had left. Dad needed me. And I seriously doubted either of my two brothers would hop on a plane right now, wherever they were, to come to the city and help us out. I had to handle the Crucible all on my own. Putting aside the dread building in the pit of my stomach, I donned a pair of jeans and a white T-shirt.

The Crucible was a super fancy, by-invitation-only, night-club in Midtown Manhattan. It was owned by one of the most ruthless mafia kingpins in the city. It was more than a club. It was a place of debauchery, for lack of a better word, that catered to patrons' deepest and darkest desires. In Dad's case, gambling.

I considered my tennis shoes for a moment, then decided to go with knee-high boots. Literally, the only sexy accessory I owned. While I didn't care what their snooty bouncers thought of me, a nicer outfit might increase my chances of getting in without having to call in a favor.

At this hour, I wasn't sure if I would get a cab quickly, so I decided to get an Uber. As if the universe were trying to reward me for being a good daughter, my assigned driver was only a minute away. I grabbed my keys and headed out to meet him at the curb.

My Chelsea apartment wasn't too far from the Crucible. With light traffic, we made it to the night club in twenty minutes flat. The cool, spring air rustled pollen off the sidewalk. I smiled at the whirlwind and thought of fairy powder. Something like that would come in handy right about now. Dad's gambling addiction was getting so bad, I was willing to give fairy tales a shot.

I blinked to clear a bit of dust that made its way into my eyes and darted inside the high-rise. In the main lobby, a chandelier hovered over my head and cast twinkling lights on the Italian marble. Even though I couldn't exactly hear the music playing a few floors up, the thumping of the DJ beat trembled against the walls and the soles of my boots.

"May I help you, Miss?" The man behind the receptionist desk called after me before I reached the elevator bay.

"I'm just going up to the Crucible." I offered him a friendly smile, trying not to feel so out of place and out of my league.

"Do you have an invitation?"

"No, I'm not here to stay. I'm looking for my father."

An invitation from the Crucible owner wasn't something that was easily obtained. Only the most powerful were allowed in. Dad fell into that category not so long ago. Though in the past couple of years, after Mom passed away, Dad's position and wealth had deteriorated significantly.

I blamed Rex Valentino for all our problems. In so many ways, Rex kept Dad a prisoner in this place. Rex afforded Dad the opportunity to gamble for days at a time. He took advantage of Dad's suffering to suck him dry. Our family money was all but gone.

"I'm sorry, but I can't let you in." He tapped his earpiece as his eyes glazed over me. After a quick nod at the security camera to my right, he smiled at me. "This way, Ms. Alfera."

I opened my mouth to ask how he knew my name, but I already knew the answer. I glared at the camera and imagined the all-powerful Mr. Valentino with his arms over his chest, watching me on his monitors, studying me like I was some kind of bug. I pulled on my coat and fastened the buttons. Rex had a way of making me feel like he could see through my clothes.

Of all the other times when I had come looking for Dad, this was the first time he decided to let me in. Why now? I supposed his reasons didn't matter. I didn't have time to stand here and question his motives. Dad needed my help. When he had called earlier, he sounded sad and defeated, as if he had gone too far this time. Had he?

Given the beast that managed this club, I'd bet he'd encouraged Dad to lose even more money. I didn't have any kind of cash with me. My job as a creative director at A-List, an advertising agency, afforded me a nice apartment in the city and a few luxuries. But it would never be enough to pay for Dad's gambling debts. All I could hope for at this point was to come to some sort of arrangement with Mr. Valentino, so Dad could come home and get the help he needed.

With my heart thumping in my throat, I followed the security guard into the elevator. I had no idea what to expect of the exclusive club that took up most of the forty-story building. I pictured an old school casino with a smoky bar that smelled of bleach and cigars, like something from a goodfella's seventies movie, something cliche and cheesy.

My heart broke thinking how Dad had fallen prey to the release he was offered here. Though, I understood why he kept coming back. Two years was nowhere near enough time to get over Mom. Most days I still picked up my phone to call her. Only to realize that the number on my contacts wasn't hers anymore.

The pressure in my chest tightened like it did every time I thought of her. I inhaled and focused on the task at hand instead. I still had one parent left, and he needed me. Falling apart now wouldn't help either one of us.

"Here we are." The security guard smirked at me as if he knew something I didn't. I ignored him because his smugness was the least of my problems.

"Which way?" I glanced up when the elevator door opened and sucked in a breath. "This doesn't look like the gambling room. My father is Michael Alfera. He asked me to come for him." Somehow, I managed to keep the begging tone out of my words.

A tinge of recognition mixed in with trepidation touched his eyes. When he spoke again, the knowing smirk from before had disappeared. The name dropping had worked. Even if Dad was past his prime, in his time, he had been revered, if not feared, as much as Valentino was now.

He had met Mom when he was in his fifties. For her, Dad turned his life around and became the man she wanted him to be—good and decent and kind.

"Mr. Valentino has asked that you wait at the bar. He will find you," he said over the loud, sensual music while he held the elevator door open.

I turned my attention to the opulent scene in front of me. Not what I had expected from someone as ruthless as Rex. Shimmering chandeliers, set at intervals, hung from high above. I counted twenty of them before I decided it wasn't worth the effort. Their reflection on the massive windows made the warehouse look like it went on forever. The gold and blue accents and high-end finishes were everywhere—from the velvet furnishings and smooth marble floors to the ritzy wallpaper and shiny banister—not a single detail had been spared.

My escort patiently waited for me to peel my gaze away from the velvet sofas and club chairs grouped together where two couples were engaged in a make-out session that was about to become something else. When a nipple popped out in a confusion of arms and legs, I quickly turned away from them.

My gaze landed on the next set of couches where a woman sat seemingly by herself, eyes closed, mouth slack. By the way she kept writhing in her seat, I didn't think she was alone. Every group of people acted like they were in their own living rooms, minus the privacy. I supposed that was the purpose of it all. I wasn't a prude, but this was a bit much for me at two in the morning on a Tuesday. In six more hours, I had to be at work.

"Ms. Alfera." The security guard motioned toward the bar at the far end of the room to get my attention. "This way."

I snapped out of my trance and even managed to follow him without falling on my face. I accepted the bar stool he offered, glad to be away from the sexual commotion on the main floor. What the hell was a seventy-year-old man doing in this place? This wasn't Dad. Or, at least, not the Dad I knew.

"Ms. Alfera." The bartender set a glass of rosé in front of me.

"No, thank you."

"My apologies. I was told this was your drink. I can get you anything you want."

The wine was my go-to whenever I needed a drink, but it wasn't about that. "I'm not here to mingle. And who told you that was my drink?"

"Mr. Valentino always makes sure his guests have everything they need. It makes the experience much more memorable."

I swallowed and then started coughing. With a kind smile, the bartender pushed the glass toward me, and I took it. Maybe a little liquid courage would help. "I'm not here for any kind of experience, or whatever it is you do here." I motioned toward the multiple set of living rooms along the main floor. "I'm here to collect my father. Would you please let Mr. Valentino know I'm tired of waiting?"

"Of course." The bartender nodded and walked away.

"Wait," I called after him, but he was gone.

I fished out my phone from the side pocket of my coat and dialed Dad. After several rings, the call went to his voicemail again. No doubt his moment of clarity was gone, and he was somewhere in this building gambling away what little money he had left.

"Phones are not allowed in the Crucible," a female voice whispered in my ear. "I'm surprised they didn't take it from you on the way in."

"I'm looking for someone." I turned to meet the woman's gaze.

She had that perfect "just been fucked" hair, and her cheeks were a pretty pink. The smile on her face was bright enough to light the room. "I'm Sofie." She offered me her hand.

7

"It's my first time here. Gosh, I feel like I can finally breathe. You know what I mean? That feeling when you just get shit off your chest and then you can truly breathe?"

"I don't, actually." My lungs worked just fine. My sex life, on the other hand, was sort of on hold at the moment. I glanced down at my hands to hide my frown. My entire life had been on hold for the past two years while Mom lost her battle with cancer.

"Hmmm." She leaned on the counter suggestively. "Did you enjoy the show? Earlier?" She pointed at the spot where I was sure I had ogled her for a good five minutes.

"I'm sorry, I didn't mean to...you know. I'm not here for any of that." I shook my head several times.

"That's okay." She beamed at me. "We're moving down to room twenty, if you want to join us." She pointed left to a cluster of deep blue sofas dotted with gold decorative pillows.

My heartbeat spiked at the idea of joining her group. That wasn't me at all.

"Um, no, thanks. I'm good." I reached for my glass and took a big gulp of wine. Where the hell was Dad?

And then I felt it. His presence had a way of sucking all the air out of the room. The hair at the back of my neck prickled. Instinctively, I drew my coat closer and checked the buttons. I lifted my gaze and found his reflection on the mirrored panel behind the bar. His form was no more than a shadow as he approached the top of the grand staircase that led to what I assumed was the VIP loft. He gripped the golden banister and leaned slightly forward as if he were searching the room. Even though it was dark, I swore his gaze zeroed in on my back, willing me to face him.

8

I slid off the barstool. A part of me wanted to run out and never come back, but I still didn't know where Dad was. With a shaky breath, I braced myself and turned around. But when I did, he was gone. Did I imagine the whole thing? I had hated Rex for so long, maybe I was starting to hallucinate about him. Why did he think everyone should bow to him as if he were some kind of king? *He wasn't.* He was a criminal, a nightmare, a heartless thug who didn't care how much he was hurting Dad and me. I wanted to knock some sense into Dad for putting me in this position.

Whatever game Rex thought he had going on was over. I was done sitting around like a good girl, waiting for Dad to magically appear. He was obviously not on this floor. I pushed off the counter in a huff, pissed off that I had let this much time go by. In my defense, it was two in the fucking morning and I was beyond tired—not just from lack of sleep but from my entire life.

Intense heat hovered over me before his hand brushed my lower back. My body jerked in surprise and raw nerves because, this time, I was sure Rex was real and standing right behind me. He'd come out of nowhere and now had me caged in against the barstool. I reached for my wineglass and downed the rest of it. Great, the man had officially driven me to drink.

"Shhh." His long fingers appeared in my peripheral vision. Then the rustle of his dark suit had me thinking he had stuffed his hands in the pockets of his trousers. "Why so jumpy?"

"I'm not." I managed not to slump my shoulders or do anything else that would indicate I was cowering at his mere presence.

"How long are you going to pretend you don't know me,

Caterina?" Rex's smooth, deep voice was loud and clear over the music. When he released a breath, a puff of warm air traveled from the nape of my neck and settled between my legs.

Yet another reason why I hated Rex Valentino so much.

CHAPTER 2
Well, That's a Loaded Question

REX

"What do you want?" She fisted her hands and turned to face me.

Jesus Christ, I had forgotten how beautiful she was. Her long, dark hair fell in messy waves several inches past her shoulders and framed her high cheekbones to perfection. If I had to guess, she had been asleep when the old man called her to get her to come down to the Crucible. I switched my attention to the couple having sex across the way as I considered her question.

"That's a loaded question, love." I had a long list of things I wanted from her. The main one being her tight little body in my bed.

She squinted her eyes at me and followed my line of sight. "In your dreams. You're such a brute."

"You came to me." I raised my voice over the loud music. Maybe bringing her to this section of my nightclub hadn't been the best idea. But when I saw her over the security monitors, I couldn't resist the temptation to show her this room. "I would never make you do anything you don't want."

"I'm looking for Dad. And before you try and tell me he isn't here. You should know he called me. If you don't release him, I'll call the police."

I chuckled. I had always admired her tenacity. How had I managed to stay away from Caterina this long? For the past couple of years, since her mother died, I had tried to do the honorable thing and leave her alone. But desperate times and all that. As much as I needed to stay away from her, I also had to protect my family. And for that, I needed her.

I took in her scent before I raised my gaze to meet hers. The hate I found there wasn't anything new. Caterina Alfera had been my enemy since birth. Our parents had forever been in a constant battle for the seat at the head of the table and the power to control the Society, a hundred-year-old enclave that managed criminal activity all over the country.

"You know very well the police work for me. As for your dad? He chose to be here."

"Why did you bring me here?" She jutted her chin. "Why do you think you own everything?"

That small act of defiance made my blood stir. The urge to make her mine and control every detail of her life rushed to the surface. I reached for her wrist and pinned it to the bar counter. Her slender fingers looked so delicate and fragile under my large hand. Not that my size had ever intimidated this woman. She squared her shoulders, and somehow, her eyes managed to show more hate and disdain for me.

"The fact that I do." I waved in the general direction of the massive room we were in. "And you know why I brought you here. I had expected you earlier. Then you show up in an interesting choice of clothes, which would indicate to me you weren't here for my social function."

"That was today? I forgot." She dropped her gaze from my face down to my tuxedo jacket. "That explains the monkey suit."

"You ignored my invitation."

"I'm not your beck and call girl. You can't just summon me whenever you feel the need to." She jerked her arm away from me, and I tightened my hold on her. "Who died and made you the king?" Her breath hitched. "I'm sorry. I didn't mean that."

"That's a low blow even for you." I cocked my head to look her in the eyes. The hate there had dissipated some, replaced by pity. Caterina understood well what it meant to lose a parent. Dad had passed away last month. Technically, he was shot in the back by a coward. Now it was up to me to ensure the Society survived. "Do you truly not understand how important this is? Our families are in danger, Caterina. You can't keep pretending you don't belong with me." I gritted my teeth. Caterina had a way of putting me on edge. I inhaled and corrected my statement. "You belong with the Society, the same as me. It's time you came home."

"No." She stepped closer to me, jabbing a finger into my chest. "It's time you realize the Society is a thing of the past. Let it go. Dad did."

Something in the air shifted like a rush of raw energy that threatened to consume me. That had always been the case with her. This incessant need I had for her would have to wait though. I needed to focus on the job Dad had entrusted to me. The Society was under attack. And if Dad was right, the person behind his murder was dead set on seeing that our century old legacy died a quick death.

"That's not up for discussion." I released her arm. "You'll join the meeting upstairs."

"And if I don't?"

"I'll make you." I deadpanned. "I've never been a patient man. And you know that."

"I'm not going anywhere with you. Not until I see my father."

If Caterina saw her father now, it would absolutely break her. The old man had lost it after his wife died. His behavior was deplorable and out of control, which was why I had kept him at the Crucible. He couldn't do much harm while he was in my nightclub under my supervision.

"He's been here for the past three days. What makes you think he wants to leave?" I caved into my urge to touch her and brushed the back of my hand over her soft cheek.

"He called and asked me to come here." She slapped my hand away.

"Maybe he remembered I had called for a board meeting with all the families of the Society."

"He wants out. Let him go."

"He came to me. Now he's not going anywhere." I crossed my arms over my chest. "I'll start the meeting in one hour. I expect you and your father to be there. You want to see him? That's where he'll be." I dropped my gaze to her jeans and knee-high boots. What I would give to see her in nothing more than just those boots. "I've arranged for you to change into something more suitable for the occasion."

She huffed. "You have some nerve. I'm not your stupid doll."

"You're in my house. If you scream, no one will help you."

"What the hell does that mean?" She shuffled back.

14

Any other night, I would have loved to stay here and keep this conversation going with her. But we had more pressing matters to attend to, and Caterina needed to understand that. I bent down and threw her over my shoulder. The impact knocked the wind out of her, and that gave me time to make my way back to the grand staircase before she started kicking and screaming. I tightened my hold over her legs and climbed the steps two at a time. Luckily, the VIP loft on the second floor was mostly empty by now. The few guests that remained didn't even notice us as we crossed the room to the elevator bay in the back.

"When Dad hears about this, he'll want your head on a spike." She pushed against my back.

"I don't think so, love." I moved my hand up an inch, and she froze. "These days, your dad can't see past the blackjack table."

I hit the call button. When the doors slid open, I walked in and released her.

"You can change in the guest room." I inserted my key and pressed the dial for the Penthouse, doing my best not to dwell on the fact that Caterina had never been to my home before. "On the bed, you'll find a dress to wear. Mary Anne, my assistant, will help you."

I texted Mary Anne to confirm she had done as I requested. She responded almost immediately to let me know she had the guest room ready. Caterina spent the entire ride up to the forty-fourth floor glaring at me from her corner of the elevator car. Her cheeks had turned a pretty pink that matched her pouty lips. I shoved my phone inside my jacket and stuffed my hands in the pockets of my trousers.

15

"You always get your assistant to buy clothes for women you find downstairs and drag up to your fancy penthouse?"

"Yes. That's part of her job description." I had no idea what it meant that she was curious if I brought other women to my home.

She winced. "You're not even kidding."

"Why would I kid about that?"

A pang of excitement rushed through me when the doors slid open again, and I found myself ushering Caterina into my living room. I couldn't remember the last time I brought someone up here. Her gaze followed a path from the marble floors up to the massive fireplace that reached the top of the high ceiling.

"You live here?" She ambled toward the tall windows facing the city lights.

"I can give you a tour of my suite if you'd like." I met her in the middle of the room.

"In your dreams." She puffed out a breath. "Where's the damn dress?"

"Does this mean you're willingly coming to the meeting?"

"Isn't that the deal? I show up and you let me see my father?"

For the first time ever, Caterina and I managed to come to an agreement. The old man was right. Caterina would do anything for him. She came straight here without a second thought to her well-being when he called. She came knowing I would be here, knowing I wouldn't let her leave until I got what I wanted.

"You would do anything for your father, wouldn't you?" I walked a wide circle around her, so I could see her face.

"I'm all he has left." She put her chin in the air with a defiant flare that was so Caterina.

"That's not true."

"If you mean my brothers, you're wrong. I haven't seen them since Mom..." Her eyes filled with tears.

I made to dab her cheek, but she turned away. The late Anna Alfera had been the glue that kept the Alfera family together. Without her, her husband, two sons, and even Caterina had been slowly falling apart. I wanted to tell her that it would all be okay—that as long as she and her dad stayed with me, they'd be safe—but I doubted she would believe it coming from me.

"I thought you were in a hurry to get to this meeting." She faced me. The sadness in those green eyes had been replaced with determination and the usual hate she reserved only for me.

"Yes." I motioned toward the grand staircase. "It's through here."

For whatever reason, she didn't jerk away from me when I took her hand in mine and escorted her up the steps. Caterina's eyebrows shot up in surprise when she reached the landing that opened up to the wide hallway. My chest expanded with pride. I had never been able to impress her with anything until tonight. Her gaze lifted to the row of old, oil paintings lining the corridor walls and the intricate, wood carvings on the decorative pilasters.

I glanced down at her palm and squeezed it before I stopped in front of a large door. If only Michael had had the guts to explain to her why she was really here, we wouldn't be wasting our time with all this preamble. "Mary Anne will help you get ready and then she'll take you to your dad." I let go of her hand, but she stayed close to me. That small gesture unraveled something deep in my chest, even though she wasn't here for me. "You love your father so much you're willing to come all this way, go through all this trouble, just for him?"

"Technically, you dragged me up here. But to answer your question, yes. I would do anything for him."

"Technically, I carried you. What did he ever do to deserve such devotion from you?" Shaking my head, I inserted a gold key into the latch and turned it.

She shrugged and crossed the threshold. I leaned my shoulder on the doorframe and watched her amble toward the bed and the red dress draped over the mattress. When she reached out to touch the silky fabric, Mary Anne barged in from the ensuite bathroom.

"Perfect timing." She beamed at Caterina. "I was just getting your bath ready."

"My what?" She spun around to face me.

I reached for the knob and shut the door. The idea of Caterina naked in my house put me over the edge. I had to get out of here and focus on what I had to do. Tonight, I had to be the leader Dad needed me to be. I had to talk to the board members of the Society—the Dons of the five original crime families. I had to convince them that the only way to survive the threat hanging over our heads was to work together.

Releasing a breath, I headed downstairs, using a secret passage that linked my penthouse to the headquarters of the Society, the same place where the first Dons met for the very first time over a century ago. I played with the ring on my finger, rubbing the lion's face engraved on the platinum. If everything went well tonight, if I secured the backing of all the families, I would be one step closer to making good on the promise I made to Dad—no matter what, save the Society.

If all went well tonight, I would finally get the woman I had wanted most of my adult life. I pushed open the paneled door and strolled into a small room where my bodyguards waited for me.

"Sir," all five men said in unison and stood at attention.

"Will Ms. Alfera be joining you, sir?" Frank, my most trusted bodyguard, stepped forward, ready to escort me to the meeting room down the hall.

"She's getting ready as we speak." A smile pulled at my lips as I adjusted my cufflinks. "Is everyone still in the anteroom?" I moved on to smooth out my tuxedo jacket and a waft of Caterina's perfume clinging to the fabric hit me square in the face. *Fuck. I had to stop thinking about her.*

"Yes, sir. No one dared leave without seeing you first. But they're growing restless." Frank met the men's gazes one by one and they all confirmed with a single nod.

"Let's not make them wait any longer." I gestured for him to get the door. As soon as I walked onto the main corridor, my phone buzzed with a message from Mary Anne.

Mary Anne: I'm sorry. Ms. Alfera escaped.

I saw red as I typed a quick response.

Me: Find her!

Son of a bitch. I should've known Caterina would pull something like this. She would never lift a finger if it meant I would benefit from it. She had gone too far this time. This was too important. If playing the nice guy hadn't worked, now she would have to deal with the ruthless king. I was done asking.

"Bring the old man to me." I practically spat the words. "And then get her."

CHAPTER 3
You're Not My Prisoner

Caterina

After Rex left me in the guest room with his assistant, I had to play along. Though odd and so out of place, the bath was nice. In the short five-minute soak Mary Anne allowed, the essential oils and warm water did wonders for my tired muscles. She was extremely deft and patient as she got me into the dress and ushered me to the vanity seat to work on the updo.

"This quick twist is all we have time for tonight. We can talk about how you like to wear your hair later. I'll be more than happy to help."

The what? Why in the world would I need her to do my hair after tonight? I opened my mouth to ask, but then decided against it. Obviously, Rex had no intention of letting Dad go. And now that I was here, he planned to keep me here too.

"I'll get your shoes." She smiled and returned to the bathroom.

What kind of assistant was she anyway? How did she not

see how weird this whole situation was? I didn't get a chance to ask her any of that because the minute she left me alone, I made a run for it. Without a keycard, the elevators wouldn't work for me, so I headed for the stairwell, which led me to a wide corridor.

My God, this place was a freaking maze. I opened a paneled door that turned out to be just a cubby hole or closet. The Society had built this place to be like a modern-day castle, full of secret doors and passages. Rex's penthouse looked like it had been recently renovated, along with the nightclub floors, but the rest of the property still had that old world feel.

I ran my hands along the faded wallpaper, looking for another way out in this massive corridor. When I made to take another step, my gown caught on a nail sticking out from one of the baseboards. I yanked at the gown and kept going, wishing I'd had time to change back into my jeans before I escaped.

Escaped?

This was always the thing with Rex. Every time I had any kind of interaction with him, my entire life got turned upside down. Three hours ago, I was sleeping in my bed. Now I was on the run from a mafia kingpin, dressed like I was on my way to some fancy ball.

But I didn't have time to worry about my clothes or sleep. I had about a handful of minutes before Rex checked his cameras and figured out exactly where I was. I had to get to Dad and get him out of here. Screw Rex's mobster meeting. Maybe I didn't know Rex all that well, but I knew one thing for sure—everything he did was for him, for some sort of gain.

Rubbing my cold arms, I stopped to try and figure out a plan. The building had seemed so much warmer with Rex next to me. My skin still tingled where he had touched me— so high on the back of my leg. A few more inches, and he would've cupped my butt cheek. Tears stung my eyes.

I hated him. I hated that I couldn't think straight when he was around. I hated how infuriatingly confident he had been that he would get everything he wanted from me tonight—like going to his stupid Society meeting.

A cold draft seeped through the carpeted floor, and my bare feet cramped in protest. I uttered a bunch of profanities directed at Rex as I tried every panel and doorknob along the hallway. I had yet to find the stairs.

From the elevator ride, I knew I was forty-four floors up. It would take a while to get to the street level, but it could be done. I had to find Dad and take him home. This place wasn't for him. He was too old and too sick to be here this long. Hadn't Rex said Dad had been at the Crucible for days?

"Caterina, stop." Rex appeared out of nowhere at the end of the hall. "Why won't you ever listen to me?" He sauntered toward me. When his gaze zeroed in on my feet, he winced. "You'd put yourself in danger just to get away from me?"

"Being barefoot is hardly any danger."

"I wasn't talking about the shoes. I was talking about what's out there, waiting for you. I've told you many times before. I would never hurt you."

"And yet, that's exactly what you're doing by keeping me here."

"What? I merely asked for one hour of your time. You're not my prisoner. And neither is your dad." The edge in his tone told me he was at the end of his rope. Good. Now we could both lose our minds in this crazy labyrinth of secret walls. This was exactly why I stayed away from Rex as much as possible. He wanted to control everything.

"Where is he then?"

"Downstairs. Gambling. I was on my way to get him when I got Mary Anne's text." He reached into his pocket, then put his phone to his ear. "I found her. Take Michael Alfera to the library. We'll meet you there." He didn't wait for confirmation before he tapped on the screen.

When Rex gave orders, he expected them to be obeyed. That small reminder of who I was dealing with sparked a wave of anger that settled in the pit of my stomach. On a normal day, I was what anyone would consider a nice girl. But Rex made this other side of me come to the surface. Even now, all I wanted to do was slap the knowing smile off his face.

"I'll have Mary Anne bring your shoes." He stood inches from me. "You look stunning in that dress."

Prickling goosebumps blossomed across my chest every time Rex puffed warm breath in my direction. Did he run here? Not that I cared. "I look ridiculous." I made to push him out of the way, even though I had no clue how to get to the library.

He grabbed my wrist and slammed my back against his front while his other hand held me by the waist. Raw. Everything about him was just raw—raw energy, raw testosterone, raw want. "I'm trying to be patient for you," he whispered in my ear. "It's just a meeting. I need you here tonight."

"Mary Anne let it slip that I was to stay here for more than just hours. I don't trust you. You're planning to do something with Dad."

I struggled, and that gave him reason to hold me tighter. His lips brushed the side of my cheek, and I squeezed my legs

23

together, trying my best not to melt into him. "You're right. Tonight's meeting is way more than that. This isn't some happy family reunion."

"Dad gave all this up years ago. I live a normal life, Rex." I inhaled. I hadn't meant to say his name aloud. It was like invoking the devil to come to me and give me anything I desired.

Problem was Rex's favors came at a very high price; everyone knew that, which was why I made it a point not to get near him to begin with—let alone ask for his help.

"I have a job. An apartment that's all mine. Friends that don't know that criminal families exist, that you exist. You're pulling us back into something we don't want."

"I know." He exhaled and leaned ever so slightly into me. "I let you be for as long as I did because I knew you didn't want this life. But it's no longer up to me. You're not safe out there. It's time to come home."

"You don't need me. You want me here as some sort of prize. Everything you do, you do for you. I'm not a thing."

"Everything I do, is to keep our families from going extinct." His long fingers cradled my shoulders. "Don't move."

I wanted to get away from him because my body was seriously sending him mixed messages. First, he had to understand that the desire unfurling at my core had nothing to do with him and more to do with general sexual frustration. I was glad he didn't see my eyes flutter closed as I took in his musky scent. Danger, power, and sex oozed from him.

"Ha." I sucked in a breath. When I glanced down, I spotted the sparkling diamond necklace he had rested on my chest. "I don't need a leash. I'll go to your stupid meeting."

His deep chuckle did things to me I wasn't ready to

acknowledge. He gripped my shoulders and made me turn to face him. *Fuck me.* I glared into that intense blue gaze of his under full brows. I'd forgotten how young and beautiful he was. Shit. I shouldn't have made eye contact. When I realized my mouth had been opened this whole time, I swallowed hard and closed it.

"It's just a necklace, love. Jesus, you won't even accept a gift from me?"

"Why would I?"

He inhaled deeply, and his shoulders relaxed a little. "Earlier you said you'd go with me and then you ran off. Can I trust you'll stay put this time?"

"I didn't promise before."

"Are you willing to pinky swear now?" A smile pulled at his lips.

"Will you take me to Dad?"

"How could I not when you ask so nicely?" He shifted the heavy diamonds on my clavicle so they would be centered.

Everything had to be exactly how he said. I had to be dressed in the dress he said. And decorated just like he wanted. And that right there, snapped me out of my trance. I pushed away from him. "Then I promise. Let's go." I gestured to my left. "I'd like to see Dad in this lifetime."

"This way." He motioned to the opposite end. "You were so close to finding the exit."

I rolled my eyes and stalked past him. In two strides, he moved in front of me and opened a hidden door that led to yet another stairwell. My heart drummed faster when I realized that in the half hour I had to escape, I never really left his penthouse.

When we reached the floor below us, his men were

waiting for us. One of them nodded to Rex and ushered me down the corridor to a massive double door. This level had more of a mobster feel to it with its carmine silk walls and opulent furnishings.

A long time ago, when I was a teenager, Dad brought me here to meet an old friend, Rex's dad. That single trip had been an exciting adventure to me. I got to see this underworld full of mobsters and kings—a world that, to me, only existed in Dad's bedtime stories.

"Dad." I rushed into the library and hugged him.

"I knew you'd come." He hugged me tight then put me at arm's length. "I'm sorry for putting you through all this tonight."

"What happened, Dad? I thought you said you were done with the families and the Crucible." I gestured toward the elaborate fireplace taking up most of the library, the uphol-stered club chairs, and the chandeliers. Everything in this room screamed mafia. "Were you here gambling?" A part of me wanted him to say no. That he stopped by for a drink and Rex made him stay.

"Rex made me see reason. I have no other recourse. You'll see."

"So, he's making you do this? Did he make you call me to get me here?" I realized I was looking for reasons to blame this whole night on Rex. Anything was better than dealing with Dad's gambling situation.

"I was already downstairs playing." He cleared his throat. "I needed cash. And well, you know how that works."

Of course, the two things were connected. Rex wanted me here to play the ally. Dad wanted money, so Rex was happy to oblige in exchange for a small favor—call me at one in the morning and guilt me into coming here. I should've known.

"Well, I agreed to stay for the Society meeting. But as soon as that's done, we're leaving. I don't care what Rex wants. Can I have your word, please?" I wrapped my arms around his shoulders. The tuxedo he wore was freshly pressed and fit him like a glove. No matter his age, Dad would always have this aura of power around him. If he hadn't retired, he would be at the head of the table tonight, not Rex. "Did Rex send you clothes too?"

"No, I sent for these." He patted my hand. "You worry too much, Bells. Someone your age should be out there having fun in the city."

I glanced down at my hands at the mention of Mom's name for me. She named me Caterina Isabella, only to call me just Bells. I missed her. I missed my brothers. I missed having a family. "Have you heard from Massimo and Enzo?"

"No." He shook his head. "They're still mad at me. I don't think they'll ever forgive me."

"Mom's death wasn't your fault. You did everything you could. And they know that." I offered him a warm smile. "Come sit down. I haven't seen you in days. How are you doing?" I ushered him to a chair facing the roaring fire. Now that I had found Dad, this building was starting to feel familiar, not as cold.

"You know what I've been up to." He pointed toward the wine cart.

I stood and poured him a whiskey neat. "You still haven't said you'll leave with me."

"It's complicated, dear."

"If you're in trouble, you need to tell me." I set his drink on the side table and kneeled next to him. I couldn't lose him too. I'd lost too many people in the last two years.

"I owe the Crucible some money. Nothing I can't handle. I just need a few more days." He took a long sip of liquor.

"The Crucible? You mean Rex." I shot to my feet and paced the length of the small room. "He told me you weren't his prisoner. You can leave if you want."

"I'm more like collateral." He seemed defeated.

Dad wasn't the giving-up type. Our family always stuck together. Massimo and Enzo seemed to have forgotten that, but I still believed we could overcome anything. Whatever the amount, I was sure we could get the money together. The name Alfera still carried weight in this city. I could go to the bank and take a mortgage on the apartment Mom bought for me. That alone would be close to a million, if I really pushed it —begged.

"How much, Dad?"

Earlier tonight, Rex seemed willing to come to some sort of an understanding with me. He had his plate full with whatever the Society was going through. Dad's debt had to be nothing compared to his other problems. If I had to be honest, I had never seen Rex this worried. He was still an insufferable, confident bastard, but something had really disturbed him.

"One million," Dad croaked.

I spun around so fast the room swayed a little. "Tell me you're joking. How is it possible to lose that much?"

"The days are long. Don't worry about that. I'll stay here until I figure something out. I still have a few aces up my sleeve, Bells. Don't let the wrinkles on my face fool you." He raised his glass to me and then knocked it back.

"No. You asked me to come get you. You're coming home

tonight. Rex will have to wait for his money." I paced the room again.

Rex. Always Rex standing in the way, making my life miserable. Why would he let Dad's account run so high? He had to know Dad would have to forfeit on his debt. If Dad was contesting the position of king, I could see why Rex would set this trap for him. Someone as controlling as Rex would want insurance. Was that it? But Dad didn't care about the Society. He left when I was a baby. He did it for Mom. No way would he want to come back now.

"How long do you have to make good on the payment?"

"It was due last month." Dad leaned his elbow on the armrest and pinched the bridge of his nose as if he was too embarrassed to face me.

I couldn't stand to see him like that. "You're ready to stay here as his plaything? Or worse, go to jail? Dad—" My voice quavered. "I won't let him do this to you. I promise you. I'll do anything to bring you home."

CHAPTER 4
That's Not Why We're Here

REX

Frank: We lost the Alfera brother.

I squeezed my phone, glaring at my bodyguard's message. I had sent a crew to look for Massimo and Enzo Alfera. They had been recently seen in Ibiza off of the coast of Spain. My men had orders to bring the two of them home. But the Alfera brothers were smart and they didn't want to be found. I had failed in that regard. At least Don Alfera was here. That was all that mattered for tonight's meeting—well, him and his daughter, Caterina.

The hushed voices from the antechamber next door filtered through the thin walls. I smiled at Dad's family ring on my finger. Bringing everyone together here tonight had been hell, but I had done it. The message I had for them was disturbing and almost impossible, but this was the job.

For as long as I could remember, Dad had wanted the Society to be what it once was. We were the protectors of this city. But over time, greed took hold of every member until hate was all that was left. Dad had a plan to make things better. And then he got shot. I ran a hand over the red leather of Dad's old chair and swigged my whiskey. Was he right in thinking Caterina was the key to get what we wanted? Peace.

"Everyone's gathered, sir." Aaron, the bodyguard assigned to Caterina, stepped into my line of sight holding my tuxedo jacket.

"And the Rossis?"

"They're here as well. The woman is pregnant, sir."

I stood and let him help me into my jacket. "Maybe arranged marriages aren't all that bad."

"She hates him."

I chuckled. "Let's get on with it."

Aaron rushed to the door to hold it open for me. I strode across the now empty antechamber and entered the board-room. Everyone froze, and I hoped it was because they understood the gravity of the situation. I called for this assembly because we were under attack.

I glanced around the room to make a quick inventory. All families but the Gallos were here. Santino Buratti was here representing his father tonight since he was too ill to leave his home. Signoria Vittoria Salvatore had brought her niece Giulia. The older woman was as fierce and strong as an ox, but eventually, she would need to find a successor. I doubted the wide-eyed girl clinging to her side was the answer.

On the opposite end of the room, Chase and Mia Rossi stood at attention. They were not part of the five original crime families. Though Chase's grandfather had tried time and time again to be invited to join the Society. No one had ever been invited before because we didn't need to. That changed tonight, and old man Rossi was about to get his wish.

My gaze zeroed in on Dad's chair at the head of the table. The lion's head carved on the crest rail sent a surge of adrenaline through me. If these walls could talk, they would speak of simpler times when mafia families represented something else. I glared at the ashtray sitting on top of the society's crest. Gritting my teeth, I pushed it aside and met Signoria Vittoria's cold stare. She nodded once in understanding.

The emblem representing the five original crime families was carved on the table to remind us of our mission—fac fortia et patere, do brave deeds and endure.

"Where is he?" I asked Aaron.

Without the Alfera family, the assembly couldn't begin.

"He's on his way up. There was a situation downstairs. But it's resolved."

"Is she with him?" I adjusted my watch.

"Yes, sir. Everything is as you requested."

The double doors opened again and they both made their way toward me, to their place at the right side of the table, next to me. When I met Caterina's gaze, she glared at me with renewed hate.

"He's here. I hope you're happy."

I'd thought we had made a bit of progress earlier tonight. She had accepted my gift without complaint, and even put on the high heels that matched her dress. She truly was a vision. Her presence was soothing to me. I no longer cared if I was being a selfish asshole. I needed her here.

"Yes, Caterina. This makes me happy." I waited while she helped the old man into the chair to my left.

I waited another minute until everyone found their assigned seats. The Salvatores at the other end, the Rossis to my left. And the Burattis beside them.

"I believe the first time we were gathered like this; our families were still smuggling rum." I chuckled. "I appreciate you making the time to come here tonight."

"Get on with it, Rex," Signoria Vittoria said in her smoker's voice. "If it'd been up to me, I wouldn't be here, boy."

I clenched my jaw at the off-handed insult. At twenty-eight, I was hardly a boy, but what she meant was that the king's chair was too big for me. "Maybe this will be of interest to you, Signora Vittoria. As of last night, the entire Gallo family has been wiped out. Even the bastards."

"The Big 5 is now down to four." Santino twirled his family ring around his finger. The wolf's head encrusted on the platinum was the only thing that made it different from mine. He rose to his feet. "Is that why we're here, Rex? You could've sent an email and saved us all the aggravation."

"Sit down, Santino." Signora Vittoria's tone was full of warning. Not that Santino cared. He stood his ground as his gaze shifted from hers to mine.

"No, that's not why we're here, Santino. The society has been around for a long time. In one night, we lost the entire Gallo family. I brought you here to call a truce, which will stay in place until we figure out who's trying to wipe us out."

"A truce? Like what? We work together, one big happy family. No, thank you." He leaned on the table, furrowing his brows. "I'll take my chances. I work alone."

The room erupted into a cacophony of angry voices and frantic questions as everyone left their seats and congregated near the door. This was not how I thought this conversation would go. I stormed to my feet and glanced at Caterina. The terror in her eyes made my stomach churn.

The Gallo family was third in line in the Society succession. If someone was planning to take my place, they would come after her family next; even if Michael was now retired, her brothers had never left. Did she even understand the danger they were in?

I wanted to tell her that I would never let anything happen to her, but I doubted she would believe me. Before I could stop myself, I reached for her hand. Her entire body jerked as if I had given her an electric shock, before she yanked her arm away.

"There's a traitor in our midst. If you leave, I'll assume you're it. I'll have no choice but to retaliate. The bylaws are clear on this. Someone betrayed the Society, and I intend to find out who. There are only two sides to this coin. Which side are you on?"

In the next breath, several bodyguards burst through the doors with guns out as they found their bosses. This fucking assembly was over, and I had accomplished exactly nothing—if I assumed inciting panic was nothing.

"I just told you someone wants us dead. And this is your solution? Shoot the remaining Society members?" I nodded to one of my bodyguards.

He immediately left his post protecting me and went to stand next to Chase, while a second guard took Mia through the secret exit behind her to get her out of harm's way. I didn't want the Rossi family shot before they had a chance to hear my proposal. I needed all the allies I could find. Chase and Mia were not part of the five original crime families, but with the Gallos gone, someone had to take on the empty chairs. We still had a fucking business to run.

When I turned my attention to Caterina, she was gone. I grabbed the tumbler in front of me and downed the rest of the whiskey. She didn't trust me, and I couldn't blame her for that. *Fuck me.* I should've told the guards not to let her leave. But she wasn't my prisoner. Why did I think Michael would use the time he had with her in the library to explain things to her? I should've known he would be too much of a coward to tell her the truth.

Chase stayed behind while everyone scattered into the waiting room and then the hallway. I motioned for Aaron to go after Caterina. Now that she knew what was at stake, she had to see that leaving the Crucible was a mistake.

"Where the hell is my wife?" Chase turned to face me.

I nodded to my remaining guard. He promptly left the room and shut the door behind him.

"I read your file. Your grandfather raised you outside of all this. Soon you'll learn that relationships will get you killed." I had assumed Chase and Mia hated each other like Aaron had said. But now I could see how much he cared about her.

"Why did you bring us here? This isn't our fight."

Of course, he wouldn't see it as such. According to what my guys were able to dig up about Chase Rossi, he and his grandfather had recently reconnected. In a matter of days, the old man had arranged a marriage with a crew boss from Jersey, and in doing so, he managed to take control of those crews without bloodshed. Now his grandfather was dead, and Chase was in charge of the family business. I needed to know that the New York and Jersey factions understood they still answered to me.

With Society members turning up dead, I didn't have time to deal with the lower factions. Though I was more than prepared to bring the fight to their back yard if they tried to go off on their own.

"As of tonight, it is."

"What?" His gaze cut to the door, as if he was dying to chase after Mia.

"Isn't this what Jax Rossi, your grandfather, wanted? A seat at the table for the Rossi family?"

"And if I refuse?"

"No one's ever refused." I shrugged.

He didn't need to know that no one had ever gotten this offer before. Keeping the Society in one piece was all I cared about. If that meant making Chase a Don, so be it.

"What exactly are you proposing?"

"Jax had our protection. Whenever things didn't go his way, we'd step in... quietly. We can continue to do that for you. But I need a favor in return. Find the assholes who are doing this to us, the ones who killed the Gallo family."

"Why them and not you?" Chase asked.

He did understand the underlying issue here. Why go after one Don and a bunch of soldiers when they could've come after me and really broken the Society apart? Tonight's shitshow of a meeting showed me how fractured we were.

Each family worked independently and focused only on their particular industry. The Valentino's, my family, was entrusted to run the Society and ensure the Dons acted in a way that benefited all of us. Problem was, they didn't see me as their king, like they did with Dad. The assholes coming after us knew that. Killing me would've gotten them nothing.

"What if I can't find who's trying to kill you all?"

"We all die." I knitted my brows.

"You mean you die. I just got here."

"The Society has been in place this long because even though we hate each other's guts, we understand one thing.

We stand together, or we don't stand at all. Don't let their theatrics fool you. Once they see this for the very real threat that it is, they'll come back."

"That means shit to me. You'll find that my grandfather and I are very different people."

"If I didn't know that already, you wouldn't be here. Jax was never going to be one of us." I ambled to the bar cart near the fireplace, poured two drinks, and set one on the table for him.

"No, thanks." He waved his hand in dismissal.

He didn't want to do this for me because he didn't trust my family. But if trust was the only thing holding him back, that meant he had some sort of clue as to where to begin digging. My life was this side of fucked up if an outsider was the only ally I had left—a reluctant ally, but a friend, nonetheless. I hoped I wasn't wrong about him or his wife.

"You start tomorrow."

"You can't expect me to solve this for you. It doesn't work like that."

"I need people like you and Mia on my side. If the Society goes under, chaos will ensue. This country's economy needs us. It may not be apparent to you, but we're the ones keeping the peace. We're the good guys, Rossi." I stuffed my hands in the pockets of my trousers and let him study me.

"So, you want us to pledge our loyalty to you?"

"That would be step one."

"As long as we can continue to do business, you don't have to worry about the New York or Jersey factions." He met my gaze.

"Good. You'll also need to take over for the Gallos."

He slow-blinked as if this honor I'd just bestowed upon

him was a burden. His grandfather had spent a lifetime begging my dad for this opportunity. Whatever his reasons, I didn't care. The Society was at a pivotal moment. Now more than ever, we had to stick together.

"I'll see you around." He fisted his hands and made his way toward the antechamber.

When the door shut behind him, I grabbed his crystal glass off the table and threw it across the room. It hit the built-in bookcase, and glass splattered all over the antiques and leather-bound books. If Caterina had stood by my side during the assembly like she was supposed to, the outcome would have been much different. Everyone would have seen that we needed to combine our resources and find the sons of bitches doing this to us.

I was done playing nice with Michael. The time for him to hold up his end of the bargain was now.

I grabbed my phone from the inside pocket of my jacket and called Frank. Was I ready for another round of hatred from Caterina? No, I sure as hell wasn't, but we needed to discuss a contingency plan that included some kind of security for her. Whether she liked it or not, she was back into the fold. Maybe she hadn't noticed yet, but her father had already given up. The old man only cared about his own grief.

After the fifth ring, the call went to voicemail. What the fuck? I glared at the screen. Frank would have to be dead not to take my call. My heartbeat picked up the pace as I rushed out the door. A myriad of scenarios went through my head. Most of them included Caterina getting hurt. If that happened, I didn't know what I would do. I took the private elevator to the lobby to see if security there had seen him.

The doors opened, and I immediately found Frank on the

floor with a gash on the side of his head. "Mr. Valentino." He mumbled, sitting up against the wall.

"What the hell happened? Who did this?" I sat on my haunches next to him.

He winced. "She did."

"What do you mean?"

"After the assembly, Ms. Alfera mentioned her Dad wasn't feeling well and that she was taking him home. He looked pale and did look like he needed medical help. I only wanted them to wait a minute so I could consult with you. When I caught up to them, she swung around and hit me with one of the lobby busts. She took me by surprise. She didn't even wait to see what I wanted. I'm sorry." Frank leaned forward like he was about to pass out.

"We'll deal with that later. Let's get you something for that." I pointed to his injury and stood.

Jesus fuck. Was the old man really sick or was he just hoping to delay the inevitable? I fished out my phone and called the number for my security detail to fill them in on what had happened in the lobby. "Get someone to take Frank to the hospital. He's going to need stitches."

"Yes, sir." Aaron answered on the other end of the line. "I'm getting on the elevator now. Should I dispatch a team to Ms. Alfera's apartment?"

"No, leave it to me."

It was painfully obvious that she wanted nothing to do with me or the Society. I was done chasing after her. If I learned anything tonight, it was that Caterina would never be mine. Not in the way I wanted her to be. But this entire situation wasn't about us anymore. The threat hanging over the Society was bigger than all of us.

After I hung up, I called my lawyer. It was high time the Alfera family realized I wasn't playing. My lawyer picked up after the third ring, even though it was close to four in the morning. Shit. At some point, I had to get to bed and sleep. But this couldn't wait.

"Mr. Valentino, how can I help you?" he asked with a tinge of alarm in his tone.

"Michael Alfera broke his end of our agreement." Technically, he had broken more than one contract, but the money he owed the Crucible was the only tangible deal I could act on. "I'm ready to collect on his debt. Make the arrangements. I want this resolved by morning." I considered for a minute how Caterina might react to seeing her father go to jail at his age, then added, "Make sure the police are involved."

CHAPTER 5
You Know How It Is

CATERINA

"I'm not as ancient as you think. I can walk just fine on my own." Dad motioned for me to lead the way to my Chelsea apartment. For a minute back at the Crucible, I thought he was going to pass out.

At seventy-five, maybe Dad wasn't that old. But he seemed to have aged twenty years since Mom passed away. He stepped onto the curb with his gaze fixed on the front entrance of my building.

The loft style property had once been an olive oil factory that had been renovated into high-end residences. The main lobby had a receptionist desk to the right and a set of elevators on the left. Nothing fancy like Rex's building, but it was home.

Mom had bought me this place for my twenty-first birthday—an over-the-top gift even for the wife of a former mobster, but now I understood why she had done it. She wanted me to have something that was outside Dad's world, something the Society couldn't touch, something that was all my own.

Of course, her efforts had been in vain because now, I was going to have to get a mortgage to pay off Dad's debts. Mom had planned for everything, except how to make Dad want to stay alive after she was gone. I inserted the key and pushed the door opened.

"The spare bedroom is through there." I pointed down the hall on my left. "You remember."

"I do." He patted my cheek, then stalked to the exposed red brick wall with the small window facing the courtyard. The place had an artsy feel to it that reminded me of Mom every day. No doubt Dad felt her presence here too. He turned to face me. "I need to rest tonight, but tomorrow, we need to talk. You and I have a conversation pending that's long overdue." The sadness in his eyes broke my heart in two.

"Dad, I miss her too."

"She wanted something different for you. Better." He smiled at the cozy linen couch and plush pillows.

"I'm happy, Dad. That's all Mom ever wanted for all of us. I have a job I love. Friends."

"I know. And now I've come and ruined all of it."

"You haven't. I can help you. We're still a family." Even if it was down to just the two of us. "Let me help you. I was thinking about maybe talking to Rex. I was going to do it tonight, but then the assembly happened, and you got sick. How are you feeling?"

"Better. We'll talk about it in the morning. Right now, I need to sleep." He ambled over to the bedroom.

Numb, I made my way to the sofa and collapsed in a heap of tired bones and red fabric. What an insane night. My eyes fluttered closed, and instantly images of Rex's intense blue eyes flooded my mind. What a hateful man to think he could keep Dad in his nightclub like some kind of expensive necklace.

"Arggh." I screamed into the decorative pillow. How the hell was I going to get the money Dad needed to free himself of Rex? Reaching behind me, I pulled down the zipper of my gown. Oxygen rushed to my lungs, and that was all my body needed to fall asleep.

After what felt like a minute later, a bang on the door startled me awake. I scrambled on the sofa, trying to get my bearings and find my phone. Shit. It was nine in the morning. I hurried to my bedroom while I texted my boss to let her know I would be late to work.

"Ms. Alfera, it's the police." A voice rumbled out in the hallway.

My head snapped up. Rex. He called the police on us? No, he wouldn't do that. Not without talking to Dad first. Dad and I hadn't talked about the particulars of his deal with Rex. All I knew was that after almost two years of incessant gambling, he had managed to burn through millions of dollars. I personally could not wrap my head around that amount. But Dad had grown up in a mobster family where excess was a way of life.

When I was born, Mom made him leave it all behind. For twenty-five years, they had been happy together. Now that she was gone, he had returned to the only thing he knew—a mobster life. Except now, he wasn't a Don.

Rex had always had a vendetta against my family. Who the hell knew why? Maybe he hated Dad for leaving the Society, something no one had ever done before. Maybe he felt threatened by Dad because he was the only one who could unseat

Rex and take over the Society. Or maybe he just wanted to make my life miserable.

Growing up, I knew of Dad's old life because he never tried to hide it. The five original families attended functions together and interacted outside of the Society. Rex was the same age as my brother, Enzo, so I got to hear all the stories. How he acted like he owned everything, even when we were in school.

I supposed knowing he'd be king one day, that he would take over the reins of the Society, went to his head. He became especially ruthless after his mother died when he was eighteen. He held a special kind of hate for me then. I never understood why. Though it was all too easy for me to return the sentiment.

By the time he finished college, he had become the Rex I knew today, powerful, merciless, and unyielding—a beast. I called him that once.

My uninvited guest knocked on the door again. My body jerked when he called my name again. Jesus. I donned a pair of jeans and a T-shirt and headed to the door before the cop woke Dad and my neighbors.

"Good morning, officer." I used my calm, business tone.

"Good morning, Ms. Alfera." A man in a worn suit and greasy head stepped in front of the cop. "I'm Jack Smith, Mr. Valentino's attorney."

Jack Smith didn't sound like a real name. I didn't care. "What is this about?"

"I'm here to ensure Mr. Valentino's assets are secured. That is, to make sure your father doesn't leave the country."

I rolled my eyes. "We both know there isn't a corner in this world where Rex wouldn't be able to find Dad. His money is safe. He will get it as soon as I can get an appointment at the bank."

Jack raised both eyebrows in surprise, as if he hadn't expected us to have a plan. He exchanged a nervous look with the cop. "I'm afraid I was not told of an extension. We're here to take Mr. Alfera into custody until payment is made."

"Do you have a warrant?"

"He doesn't need one." The cop finally spoke. "We heard complaints from your neighbors. I have reason to believe someone might be in danger."

"Ah good. You're a crooked cop. Of course." I gripped the edge of the door as I considered what a trip to the police station would do to Dad. I mean they couldn't really take him to jail for owing money. They intended to humiliate him. This level of disrespect toward Dad was uncalled for. Being a retired Don had to count for something.

"Bells. It's okay." Dad came out of the bedroom fully dressed. He looked pale and tired, like he hadn't slept all night. "Jack. Good to see you, old friend."

"Michael." Jack nodded once with reverence. "You know how it is."

"I do." A half-smile pulled at Dad's lips. He winced and his Adam's apple bobbed a few times. When he cleared his throat, he braced a hand on the hallway wall and leaned forward.

"Dad." I dropped to my knees to catch his head before it hit the hardwood floor. "Omigod." I turned to Jack. "Call 911. I think he's having a heart attack."

"Son of a bitch." Jack reached inside his coat. To my disbelief, the asshole called Rex instead.

"What the hell is wrong with you?" I ran to my room and grabbed my mobile.

The operator answered on the third ring. I gave her a quick recount of the night before and today, leaving out the fact that Dad's stress and anxiety was due to the fact that he owed a shit ton of money to the mob and that one of their lackeys was standing just outside my door ready to collect.

I spent the next twenty minutes trying to keep Dad comfortable and making sure he was still breathing. When the paramedics arrived, I went into auto pilot, nodding to their instructions and following them to where they said for me to go.

From the back of the ambulance, I called Enzo, but it went to voicemail almost immediately. Why would he not want to talk to me? We hadn't spoken since Mom's funeral. He would have to know that if I was calling, it was for a good goddamn reason. I got that they were hurting too.

Seeing Mom lose her battle with cancer took a toll on all of us. But they couldn't just leave us like this. I wiped my cheeks and started a text thread with him and Massimo. I glared at the screen while tears pelted on my words—Dad's on the way to the hospital. Please call me.

It was one thing to tell myself that Dad and I were alone in this. But knowing for sure was like a kick to the stomach. When we arrived at the hospital, the paramedics, more or less, shoved me aside while they took Dad inside. I stood there at the canopy entrance, feeling more forsaken than ever.

"Are you with Mr. Alfera?" a nurse asked me.

When I turned to face him, the sun shined in my face and blinded me. Here I had thought I would go back to my normal life after we escaped Rex's place. "Yeah."

"Is he on any medication? For his heart condition?"

His what? I didn't know Dad had a heart condition. "I don't know. He didn't say," I mumbled. A pang of remorse gnawed at my insides. Dad had sought out the Crucible because he was hurting, and I wasn't there for him long enough to even ask about his health.

"That's okay." He motioned for me to go inside the hospital. "The waiting room is through the double doors on your right. I'll come find you when we have an update."

The stench of bleach and sweat evoked a bunch of old memories from two years ago when Mom was here. I couldn't lose Dad too. I pressed a hand to my forehead and found an empty seat out in the hallway. A few minutes later, my phone rang. My pulse quickened as I put the device to my ear.

"Hello?"

"Omigod, Caterina. Are you okay? How's your Dad?" Sarah panted into the speakerphone as if she were walking and talking. Like me, she was a creative director at A-List.

"I don't know." I sobbed into the phone. Relieved to know I wasn't as alone as I had thought.

"Okay. Don't worry about the boss. She said you could take the day off. And as many days as you need to." She blew out a breath. "Jeez, I'm so out of shape. Anyway, I'm crossing the parking lot now. I'll be there shortly."

"Oh Sarah. You didn't have to come down."

"You know I did. Don't give me that. See you in a bit." She hung up.

I laughed, shaking my head at the phone. As much as I didn't want to be an imposition, it would be nice to have someone here to help keep me calm. This waiting had my nerves on edge. I had never been a patient woman, and with Dad in the mix, I was about to explode.

"I'm trying to be patient for you."

Rex's words flashed in my mind. Of course, he wasn't. If he were, he never would've sent his crooked lawyer and cop to fetch Dad. And then Dad wouldn't be at the hospital. I stormed to my feet, wishing Rex was here so I could punch him in the face.

The double doors at the end of the white corridor creaked opened. I turned around to welcome Sarah but met Rex's intense blue gaze instead. Glaring at him, I fisted my hands and I waited as he sauntered toward me with his entourage behind him. He looked even taller in the light of day—taller and lethal. When he stopped a few feet away from me, my back tensed with a mix of fear and sheer rage.

"Don't you think you've done enough?" I whisper shouted.

"I'm here to help." He stepped closer, and I got a blast of his signature scent.

Everything about him screamed confidence. Even now he stood there, looking at me as if he could patch up Dad's heart and make everything better. He should know better than anyone that power and money meant nothing in this place. Mom had had the best treatment money could buy, and it hadn't been enough. Wasn't that how it had happened with his own mother?

"You mean you came here to help yourself?" I pointed at his bodyguards. "Came to make sure Dad didn't escape the country while convalescing?"

"No. They're here for Michael's protection. He's vulnerable right now. We need to make sure no one gets any wicked ideas." He gripped my elbow, clenching his jaw. "Why did you leave?"

"You said we weren't your prisoners. Did you lie?"

"People lie when they're afraid. I don't lie, Caterina. Ever." He cocked his head to look me in the eyes. "My men will stay until your father is ready to come home. I've arranged for him to be moved to a private room."

"We don't need you." I gritted my teeth. Mainly because I knew that was a big fat lie.

"Yes, you do." He took a strand of stray hair off my face and fixed it behind my ear.

I wished I could do the same for Dad and fix his situation with Rex. Wouldn't that be a great surprise for him? To wake up and know he no longer owed Rex anything. We could be a family again. I met Rex's gaze and opened my mouth to speak, but no words came out. What would I say to him? Help us. Make Dad's debt go away. Would that be enough? Knowing Rex, he would ask for way more than a simple gesture.

"If you need anything, call me." He nodded to his men, and they dispersed.

I could only assume they had gone to guard Dad, wherever he was in this massive hospital. Of course, they knew where to find him. Of course, they had access, and I didn't. Of course, I needed Rex. He turned to leave. In a few strides, he was halfway down to the exit. It was now or never.

"Rex." I called after him.

He stopped and glanced upward. His broad shoulders in that dark suit were so out of place in the stark white hallway. When he turned, he had a satisfied look on his face. My blood boiled, and I almost told him to go to hell. But Dad's livelihood was on the line.

"Could we talk?" I stood a little straighter.

He cocked an eyebrow. "We're talking now."

"No, I mean. In private. Can I come see you sometime?" I cleared my throat and corrected myself because our conversation couldn't wait. "I mean, can I see you tonight?"

"You know where I live." He met my gaze, and my pulse quickened.

"Ms. Alfera?" the nurse from before called after me.

"Yeah." I practically spun around to face him. For whatever reason, I was out of breath.

"Mr. Alfera is awake and wants to see you." He offered a kind smile.

"Thank you." I sighed in relief.

When I turned to find Rex, he was gone.

CHAPTER 6
You Look Like a Million Bucks

CATERINA

"Were you just talking to that guy?" Sarah walked in as Rex crossed the threshold. She stared at the double doors, mouth hanging open and eyes wide. "Jeez, I think I'm pregnant."

"What?" I laughed.

"From the blast of testosterone. Wow." She pulled me into a hug, shooting glances at the empty hallway where Rex had been. "How are you doing, girl?"

"I'm good." And that was the truth. I was glad she had come here to sit with me. "Dad wants to see me. So, I think that means we're making progress."

"I'm sure it does. Go see, I'll wait here."

On the way to Dad's room, Nurse Sam explained Dad's situation. He was stable but would need open heart surgery to address the clogged arteries. I vaguely paid attention to the details of the procedure after he uttered the words "open heart."

"I'm sorry. Did you say Cabbage?" I stopped in front of Dad's window. He seemed so peaceful yet, somehow older.

"Coronary artery bypass graft, C-A-B-G." He stuffed his hands in his white coat. "Don't worry. There won't be a test on it later. All you need to know is your dad is in good hands. Mr. Valentino has already taken care of all the arrangements."

I gritted my teeth at the mention of Rex's name. I hadn't asked him for help yet. He didn't need to be interfering in my life like this—like he owned Dad. How did Rex even know who to talk to in this hospital? Dad wasn't completely ruined, living out on the street. We could hold our own. Couldn't we? Now wasn't the time to bother Dad with money questions, but we definitely needed to have that conversation. Did I need to sell my apartment? Did he still have his penthouse? Shit.

"Mr. Valentino is one of our most generous donors, we're always happy to oblige whenever possible." He motioned toward the state-of-the-art suite Dad was in.

"I'm sorry. He was restless. I had to give him a mild sedative." Another nurse came out of the room. She was an older woman in a tight gray hair bun. The kindness in her eyes put me at ease almost instantly. "The stress he's under is making things worse. Try not to wake him." She smiled. "You have a few minutes before we have to take him to run a few tests. Go home and rest. We'll text with updates." She nodded to Nurse Sam.

"We will." Nurse Sam dipped his head in agreement.

"Thank you."

"Recovery shouldn't be a problem. If we don't encounter any complications, he should be back to normal in three to four months. Let us know if you need anything. We'll be around."

They both left. I turned my attention back to Dad, bracing my hand on the window.

If.

That was a huge *if* that Mom hadn't survived. The more reason to have Dad's Rex-problem resolved by the time he came out of surgery. All I had to do was walk back into the lion's den. When I asked Rex for a private appointment, I had hoped he'd suggest we meet at his office not his home.

"He looks good." Sarah pressed a cup of coffee in my hand. "Drink."

"Thanks. How did you get in here?"

"They let me in." She winked.

"Can I ask you a super personal question?" I reached for Dad's door and shut it.

"Yeah. What's going on?" She cocked her head. The sadness in her eyes wasn't for Dad; it was for me.

Sarah couldn't possibly have the right answer for me, but I figured it would help to say the words aloud. To see if what I was planning was as crazy as I thought. Or maybe I was putting way too much stock into my own worth. Technically, I was betting on Rex's desire to see me beg and grovel. He seemed to get a lot of enjoyment out of that.

"Have you ever slept with someone for money?" I winced, bracing myself for an over-the-top reaction.

"Wait." Her eyes went wide as she pointed toward the waiting room. "Holy shit, no way. The guy from before? Did he try to hire you?"

I chuckled. "No, not at all. Of course he didn't. It was just a crazy thought."

"Do you need money, sweetie? I have some stashed away.

It won't pay for the medical bills, but it'll get you by for a few months." She wrapped her arm around me.

"We're fine. Forget I said anything." My plan was as stupid as it sounded.

She bumped her shoulder against mine. "When I was in college, I gave my boyfriend a blow job for helping me move. Does that count?" She shrugged.

"I don't know what I'm saying." I touched a hand to my forehead.

For a moment, I wanted to tell her everything—about who Dad really was, about Rex, and about the indescribably difficult situation I found myself in. But I couldn't do it. I was afraid she would get hurt for knowing too much. She was my closest friend. But this thing with Rex, I had to face it alone.

"Hey, so I have to go home and get some stuff for Dad. But thanks for stopping by. I was freaking out before."

"Don't mention it. I'm gonna get back to the office. Text if you need anything." She hugged my neck and then took off.

I sat with Dad until the nurses came in and got him. The tests needed before surgery were going to take hours, which gave me some time to get away. I walked through the maze of hallways, following the signs to the waiting room. From there, I was pretty sure I could find the way out. When I reached the ER entrance, I spotted Aaron, one of Rex's bodyguards. As soon as he saw me, he jerked into action, heading my way.

"Ms. Alfera. Mr. Valentino asked me to stay behind and drive you home."

"Of course he did." I considered making a point and tell him no. But then I would have to walk all around the medical campus to hail a cab and waste precious time. "Lead the way."

"Just here." He pointed at the black SUV parked behind an ambulance.

I climbed in the back and relaxed on the soft leather. I must've dozed off because when I opened my eyes again, we were pulling up to my building. "I'll be just a few minutes."

If Rex had bothered to send a car, I could only assume he meant for Aaron to drive me to the Crucible.

"I'll be here. Take your time." He hopped out and opened my door.

My blood pumped hard and fast through me as I rushed upstairs to get ready for my appointment with Rex. Based on what I saw at the assembly with the Society members, I could tell Rex appreciated formality and decorum. Normally, I wouldn't give a damn what he liked, but today I aimed to please him. I showered quickly and blow-dried my hair. After playing around with the tresses framing my face, I decided to use a curling iron to add a few messy waves.

I slipped into a black, cocktail dress that didn't require a bra. It was sexy without showing too much cleavage, since the spaghetti straps were adjustable. When it was all said and done, I stared at my reflection in the mirror, and my resolve crumbled. Who in their right mind would pay to have sex with me? Jesus, what the hell was I doing? I sat on the bed and dropped my head into my hands.

But then I thought about how Rex made me spend almost an hour in a room full of strangers having sex. If anything, Rex Valentino enjoyed seeing me squirm and suffer. I shot to my feet. This *had* to work. Maybe he wouldn't pardon Dad's entire debt, but enough that we could come up with a payment plan that didn't include Dad going to jail or spending any more time in the Crucible under Rex's thumb.

I painted my lips red, added a pair of lacy pumps and headed out to meet Aaron. The minute I stepped out of the building, he climbed out of the SUV and opened the door for me. "Mr. Rex will be meeting you in the boardroom tonight."

"Thanks."

Glancing out the window, I imagined Rex perched at the head of the long table in the ornate red leather chair that had to be as old as the Society was. I thought of him in his pristine tuxedo with his hand casually resting on the armrest. Before I knew it, I saw him shirtless. I blinked a few times to erase the image from my mind. I didn't even know what he looked like under his designer clothes. My pulse spiked below my navel, and I squeezed my legs together. What the hell was wrong with me? No matter what, I still hated Rex. He was cruel and ruthless and...I wasn't here for me. I was here for Dad, to solve the very real threat hanging over his head.

"Here we are." Aaron said for the second time tonight.

Like before, I jerked back into reality. Jesus, we got here fast. I shifted my body to see where we were. We had gone in through a rear entrance. The garage was fairly empty except for several racer cars and other shiny brands I didn't even recognize. At the far end, the car rolled to a stop in front of a large set of glass double doors. Inside, a huge chandelier hung from the high ceiling and sparkled on the marble floors.

"Is this Rex's private access?"

"It is." He unbuckled his seat and helped me out of the SUV. "You want the forty-third floor." He motioned for me to go ahead.

I swallowed and ambled toward the elevator bay. The ride upstairs dragged on. Every time the numbers on the screen changed, the pressure on my chest increased. This would be over soon. Whatever Rex wanted from me, he would tire quickly and then Dad and I could go back to our normal lives. And who knew, maybe one day my brothers would come around.

The elevator finally arrived, and the doors slid open. As soon as I stepped onto the carpeted hallway, Rex's voice filled the air. He was on a call. A work call? I glanced around, looking for a receptionist or someone to tell me where to wait until he was finished.

"I understand your predicament. But the purchase of that company needs to go through before the end of the month. I don't care if you have to work through the weekend to finish your due diligence. Make it happen." He tapped on the phone and then threw it on the massive wooden table in front of him.

I pushed the door to open it all the way, just as he started typing on his laptop. His long fingers hit every key with purpose and some of that impatience I had come to associate with Rex's overall demeanor. When he stopped, he reached for a manila folder, then glanced up. The look in his eyes should have sent me running, but I had come this far. I couldn't back down.

He stood. To my surprise, his tie was undone and hung loosely around his collar. His crisp white shirt was unbuttoned halfway, and his sleeves were rolled up. My gaze immediately fell to the patch of light hair showing through his undershirt. I tried not to think about the fact that I might get to see more of that tonight. Seeing him like this, he looked more like the CEO and less the ruthless, mafia king.

"Caterina. You look stunning." He stepped toward me. "One could say you look like a million bucks."

I fisted my hands. He knew exactly why I had come here

today. Why did he make me meet him here? To rub it in? His crude comment knocked sense back into me. He was right. This was a business transaction.

"How about a drink?" He motioned for me to sit to his right, the same seat I had occupied last night during the assembly. "What would you like?"

"Whatever you're having."

"Whiskey." He showed me a bottle I didn't recognize. Mainly because I knew nothing about liquor. I preferred wine.

"Sure."

He poured the amber liquid in two tumblers and stalked over to me. "How's Michael doing?"

The question threw me off because he sounded genuinely concerned about Dad's well-being. "He's going to need open heart surgery."

"I know that. I meant, how is he really doing?" He sat the glass in front of me and returned to his chair or throne, whatever he called it these days.

"He's tired." I took a long swig of whiskey.

"The last two years have been taxing for everyone." He braced an ankle over his knee and let his long fingers hang over the armrest.

His gaze stayed on me. I didn't dare look up. My brain got fuzzy every time I made eye contact with him. The minutes ticked by as I continued to sip fire water and he kept on staring. How would one start a conversation such as this? I glanced down at my freshly shaven legs and thought about how hard I had scrubbed my skin in the shower trying to feel clean again.

"Caterina."

That single sound filled the room with an electric charge. Sarah had called it a blast of testosterone. Either way, my name on his lips made my head snap up. And damn if he didn't have the bluest eyes I had ever seen. And a perfect nose to go with that chiseled jaw. And...my gaze dropped to his chest again.

He chuckled.

Crap. I glared at him.

"You asked for this meeting." He gestured for me to go on.

"Right." I stood and pretended I was at work presenting a new ad campaign to a very demanding and cruel client. "As you know, my father is in the hospital, and um, he, he doesn't have your money."

"This is not new information." He slid his elbow back on the armrest, so he could rest his temple on two fingers. The odd angle allowed him to look me up and down without moving his head.

"Right. Um." I felt naked standing in front of him like this, hoping he would put me out of my misery and just take me already. But this was part of his game. He wanted me to grovel, beg. I took another swig from my glass. When I swallowed nothing but air, I put the empty tumbler back on the table with a loud thud. "The thing is, I thought maybe you could give us an extension or reduce the amount."

"Why would I do that? I'm running a business here, love, not a charity. You know that."

"I thought we could make a deal."

A surge of courage burned through me, or maybe that was the whiskey, but somehow, I found the will to step into his circle. With shaky hands, I slipped my thumbs under the spaghetti straps of my dress, rolled them off my shoulders and let the rest of the fabric drop to the floor.

CHAPTER 7
I Don't Pay for Sex

CATERINA

His breath hitched. And then he chuckled. A deep, lewd sound that set my skin on fire, and not in a good way. I was embarrassed for thinking Rex might want to pay a million dollars to be with me. I was embarrassed because I thought he actually cared and would make an exception for us. He uncrossed his legs and spread them wide. From where he sat, he remained at eye level with my breasts.

A decent man, who had no interest in making this kind of deal with a desperate woman, would look away. Instead, he licked his lips as his gaze shifted from one mound to the other and then down to the triangle between my legs. The way he looked at me, I had to glance down to make sure I was still wearing underwear. They were still on, and to add to my disgrace, I could see the wet seeping through. Could he see it on the dark fabric?

He gripped the armrests with both hands and shook his head. There was my answer. He had seen all I had to offer, and it hadn't been enough. No doubt he had at least ten other women with way sweeter dispositions waiting for him downstairs.

"You're a real beast. I hate you." I said in a shaky voice and bent down to pick up my dress.

In a swift movement, he was out of his chair and had both my hands pinned behind me on the tabletop. The softness of his dress shirt rubbed against my taut nipples, while his hot breath traveled down my back.

He cocked his head to look me in the eyes. This close, I could see how clear and almost luminescent his eyes were. That had to be the lighting playing tricks on me. In the next beat, his pupils dilated to where almost all the blue in his irises was gone.

"So, let me get this straight." He panted a breath in my face. The whiskey lingered in the air between us. "If I were to rip your thong off of you and flip you on this table, you'd let me?"

I hadn't considered what he would do to me if he agreed to our deal. When I thought about sex, I figured it would be in a bedroom and over quickly. We couldn't possibly do something like that here where the Society members met.

"Answer."

"If that's what it would take. I'm willing to do anything to save Dad."

"Yes or no?"

I imagined him doing exactly what he had said. The images played in my mind like a runaway reel. Rex forcing me out of the one garment I had left and then pressing my chest on the cold table, while he entered me from behind. I would shut my eyes and take every one of his thrusts. Why did I not think of this before? Somewhere in the unwanted fantasy he had planted in my head, I also imagined him dotting my spine with gentle kisses.

"Answer." He repeated, his voice sounded deeper and strained. "I see I have my work cut out for me. We'll have to work on your responses."

"Yes." I said louder than I meant to.

He reached for the lacey string of my underwear and pulled until it dug into my skin on the other side. All the while he kept both my hands pinned to the table. "You'll let me fuck that pretty ass into oblivion?"

I gasped. Again, another thing I hadn't considered. He leaned into me, not touching me still, but every time his chest rose and fell along with his breaths, his shirt rubbed my front. My nipples couldn't take any more of that. I was way out of my depth when it came to Rex. I was mad at myself for rushing into this and not thinking about all the things he would do to me if he had me naked and all alone in a century-old boardroom built specifically for a bunch of mobsters.

"Answer me. Yes or no?" He ghosted his lips over my shoulder. "Those are your only choices today."

"Yes." I squeezed my eyes shut, and hot tears streamed down my cheeks. He didn't have to be so crude.

"Such a devoted daughter. To give up the virginity you have held on to for this long just to save your deadbeat of a father." He released a breath. "He doesn't deserve what you're doing for him."

"He's not a deadbeat." I glared at him. Then his words fully registered. How the hell did he know I was still a virgin? I wasn't a prude or anything. But before I went to college, I promised Mom I would wait for the right guy. I looked long and hard for someone decent, and that someone never came. Then Mom got sick and time got away from me. Ironically, it seemed I was never destined to have my first time with an honorable man. I jutted my chin up to show Rex I wasn't afraid of him. "I'm not a virgin. I'm twenty-five years old. I've done it many times. Where did you get that ridiculous idea?"

He knitted his brows. Finally, I had won a round. My answer cut him. With a loud sigh, he bent over and picked up my dress by the straps. Slowly, his gaze covered every plane of my body as he raised the fabric over me like a shield.

When he brushed the back of his fingers over my nipples, heat sprung from my belly and shot straight to my clit. It happened so fast I wasn't sure if he had really fondled me there. Up until now, he'd only touched my wrists. I took over. He didn't make room for me to cover up, not even when I elbowed him a few times trying to adjust the ties.

"I suppose there's only one way to find out." He wrapped his arms around me and pressed his lips to my neck. "You're so fucking gorgeous. And I would love nothing more than to fuck you for days until you can't walk anymore, until all you know is my name." He sucked hard on the length of my cord with uneven breaths. "I'm sure there are a lot of men out there who would gladly throw a million dollars your way just to have you for one night. But here's the problem, love. I don't pay for sex."

He ambled back to the bar cart and poured whiskey into two fresh glasses while I stood there, gasping for air and shivering now that he had removed the warmth of his body from mine. "You made me believe this is what you wanted. Was this just another one of your games? To make me suffer? Why do you hate me so much? What did I ever do to you?"

"I don't hate you." He furrowed his brows and his gaze

intensified. "I truly did not think this—" he pointed at me and the table as reference to what almost happened. "—would be your next move. I have to admit, I'm pleasantly surprised."

"Fuck off, Rex." I darted toward the entrance. This meeting had not gone how I had expected at all. If anything, and as naïve as that sounded, I thought we'd be done with the whole sex thing by now.

"No." He slammed his hand on the door and shut it with a loud thud.

I could scream for help. But who was I kidding? I was in his house. It was as he had said last night, no one would help me. I was alone in this.

When I didn't move, he continued. "You came here to make a deal with the devil. Don't back down now. Let's make a deal."

I stared him down. Though all I wanted to do was run out and crawl under my bed. Rex didn't want me. All those innuendos about sleeping with me were nothing more than lewd comments to harass me and make me feel uncomfortable.

"I have nothing else to offer you."

"That's where you're wrong. Sit down. I'm going to make you an offer that, believe it or not, you can refuse. But know that once you agree to my terms, there's no going back." He motioned for me to go on and take a seat. "So, think long and hard before you answer."

I considered my non-options. I was already here. And I had made a fool of myself in the most spectacular way. There wasn't anything he could do to embarrass me further. To be honest, I was intrigued. What could he possibly want from me? I had no money or high-end properties, which of course he knew if he also knew I was a virgin.

"Please have a seat. I have no intention of letting you leave until I show you what I really want from you."

"Show me?" My nipples perked up at his words. Apparently, my body hadn't received the memo that sex with Rex was off the table. Literally.

He glanced down at my chest and smiled. "The sooner you sit down and listen to me, the sooner you can go home and take care of things."

That set me right. *Asshole.* I shoved him away from me and strode back to my chair. Why did he have to be so hot and cold? I'd been in this room for all of ten minutes and I was already dizzy and confused. I turned to face the grandfather clock near the door and realized, I'd been here with Rex for almost two hours. What? How?

"Enough with the games. Just tell me what the fuck you want so Dad and I can get on with our lives." I sat up straight in my seat, grateful that he didn't know how uncomfortable the throbbing and wetness between my legs had become.

He sauntered to the bar cart and picked up a tumbler then a manila folder off the table and slid one item at a time across the table. I went for the drink first. All this preamble had my nerves on edge—just how Rex liked it.

"All I want from you—" he pointed a lazy finger at the file, "—is your complete surrender."

"What the hell does that even mean?" I flipped open the page and gasped.

I saw red for several beats before I recovered and stormed to my feet. Rex did too. He probably thought I was going to try and run out the door again, which I definitely wanted to do. What the fuck?

"What the fuck? I thought you didn't pay for sex."

"This practice isn't about sex." He cocked an eyebrow. "As you can see."

I didn't want to see. "Is this for real or another one of your games?"

"This is what kept me going after Mom died. After I found out about all the things I was expected to do for the Society. It helped me cope. And I think it might do the same for you. Michael is being selfish."

"Yeah, and you're more than willing to stand here and take advantage of it. How noble of you."

Rex moved my drink aside, emptied out the manila folder on the table and then spread out every single picture for me to see. I glanced upward feeling like a peeping Tom. The rest of the images were not as shocking as the first one. He had done that on purpose to get a rise out of me. Once my pulse returned to normal, I was able to see what was in front of me for what it was. A kink. More specifically, Rex's kink.

He relaxed his hip on the edge of the table and smiled. A gesture that melted the lump churning in my stomach. He tapped a finger at a page. "She asked for this. I would never ask you to do more than you can handle. This process is about trust."

I laughed. "Something you and I will never have."

"Not if we don't try." He motioned for me to look, to really look.

I reached for my tumbler and knocked it back. The burn helped me find my bearings again. For once, Rex decided not to rush me as I scanned every page. He patiently waited until one caught my eye, and I picked it up. "Tell me about this one."

"The practice is called kinbaku. It's an ancient Japanese form of bondage. It technically means tight tie, and it sort of implies *with connection.*" He lifted an eyebrow at me as if the word should mean something to me, which it didn't. "There are several terms to learn but for now, this is all you need to know."

"Kinbaku." I repeated the word.

My gaze dropped to the woman in the picture, her round hips and voluptuous breasts. I glanced down at myself and what I had recently offered Rex. No wonder he wasn't interested. My eyes watered when I realized how far off the mark I had been. The blonde looking up at me oozed confidence and a sense of peace. The rope binding her legs together had an intricate series of flowers all from the same tie. In truth, it was a work of art that must have taken hours to do.

"You did this?" I ran a finger over the sequences stacked between her legs that met at her apex. For lack of a better word, they were perfect in execution. Something that struck me as so Rex. He was exactly this, a perfectionist, and a control freak.

"I did."

"How long did it take?"

"Two hours." He raised his hand before I could protest. "Not what I'm expecting you to do. These women have been practicing for years. It's a skill." The half-grin that touched his lips made him look younger. And like the women in the pictures, he appeared content and at peace when he spoke.

"Why me?" I lifted my head toward him.

He perched a leg on the table and crossed his arms over his chest. Oh, he was enjoying this. His gaze found mine. I stood my ground and stared back for what felt like hours. And just when I thought I couldn't handle any more of his scrutiny, he answered.

"I think your surrender would be sweet. The fire in your eyes begs me to put you at ease. I can do that for you. If you can find a way to trust me."

"You're doing this for me now?" I braced my hands on my hips.

That small gesture made him lean forward and regard me with intensity in his eyes. Shit. That was it. Every time I defied him, he thought it was a direct assault. He thought that was me daring him to control me. I was a challenge for him. What could be more satisfying than to tie down the only daughter of his enemy? My father, the man who at any point could unseat Rex from his so-called throne.

"For the both of us. So, here's the deal I'm willing to make with you. And all you have to do is say yes." He rose to his feet and closed the space between us. "I will pardon your father's debt and even recover all the properties he has lost in the past year. He will have the freedom to come back to the Society or not. His choice—for real this time."

"And in return?"

"You become mine. All mine." He placed his large palm on the woman in the photo, the red head with stars in her eyes. "I want your complete and utter surrender."

"For how long?"

CHAPTER 8
Did That Hurt?

Rex

"The terms of your stay are negotiable." I stuffed my hands in the pockets of my trousers while I tried to reel in my shallow breathing to regain control. I had to stay focused and not give into all the things I wanted to do to her.

Jesus Christ. Caterina had a way of unhinging me. The hate and the fire in her green gaze had haunted me for years. Now I also had to contend with her perfect tits and those mouth-watering nipples begging to be sucked.

Why would she go there? When she asked for this private meeting, I had assumed she was ready to do whatever I asked. I should've known she would come prepared with an offer of her own. And fuck me, if I didn't want to send it all to hell and take her up on it.

For all my honorable intentions, if I could call them that, I hadn't resisted the urge to peek inside her panties. Something I realized now was a complete mistake because I couldn't stop thinking about her bare sex, the smell of her arousal, and her plump outer lips. If she asked me for sex again, I didn't know if I would have the strength to refuse her again. I still couldn't figure out how I had managed it before. Her pussy was like a ripe fruit, and I wanted nothing more than to...

"As in a contract?" The quiver in her voice stopped me from spiraling down into yet another Caterina fantasy.

She ventured another step toward the table and then squeezed her legs together. Staying away from her would be hell, especially after she moved in with me. But this was too important for me to taint it with a tumble around a boardroom table. I rubbed the stubble on my cheek to hide my smile and chase the filthy images flooding my mind.

"Yes, but before I show you." I walked around the table and picked up my portfolio. "We'll both sign a non-disclosure agreement." I shuffled through my folders until I found the one with Caterina's name on it.

"If you're so embarrassed about your kink, maybe you should, you know, not do it." She glared at the papers I set in front of her.

"I'm the owner of a sex club, Caterina. This agreement is for your protection. And the peace of mind of all my clients." I waved in the general direction of the photos I had chosen to show her.

Her lips parted slightly. "These women paid you to do this to them?"

"Of course not. At the time these pictures were taken, they were my submissives." I sat down and motioned for her to do the same. She seemed more at ease when we were at eye level. "A lot of them are still members of the Crucible. They're no longer with me, but they continue to, for all intents and purposes, be my clients."

I refilled her glass, and she sipped from it absently as she read the non-disclosure agreement. Since I took over as leader of the Society, I had closed many deals. None of them were as important as this one.

If Caterina said yes tonight, I would finally have everything I ever wanted within reach. With her by my side, the Society could not only survive its current threat, but also thrive and flourish as something new, something more relevant to the current times.

"What would we tell people?" She glanced up. "The families are going to think something is up if all of the sudden I move into your palace." She waved her hand in the general direction of the built-in cases.

"They can think whatever they want. As long as you don't tell them what you're here to do." I leaned forward and braced my arms on my knees. "What we do behind closed doors is none of their business."

"What am I going to tell my friends? I have a job to go to."

"You can quit."

"What a chauvinistic thing to say. I'm not going to drop my entire life just to please you. I'm not a toy." She glared daggers at me.

The urge to take her upstairs and tie her down rushed through me. I wasn't lying before when I said I was doing this for both of us. I needed her to give into me. I needed her to be mine. I needed to control everything in her life. That was on me. Kinbaku afforded me a way to do it that wouldn't be harmful to her. If I could just have her for one hour a day, this incessant need I had of her would subside to a manageable level.

"I never said I was prince charming. I know what I'm

asking is beyond anything a person should ask of another, which is why I need your consent—in writing. I promise I will not make you agree to anything you can't handle."

"I can deal with not telling people. I could make up some story about moving in with my estranged cousin." She sat back, looking satisfied with herself.

"We're not telling people we're related because we're not. I don't lie, remember?"

"No, you don't. You're just asking me to lie on your behalf."

"I'm asking you not to divulge the details of our sessions."

"Sessions? That's what we're calling them?" She brushed her hand over one of the photos, then took it away with a tinge of fear in her eyes.

I wanted to hold her and tell her there was nothing to be afraid of. But until she learned to trust me, no number of words or holding would convince her of anything different. This was Caterina Alfera after all. The most stubborn and indelible woman I had ever met.

But tonight, all I had on my side was hope and I had to go with that. I reached inside the pocket of my briefcase and retrieved a three-foot rope. I figured anything longer would scare her off.

Her body jerked in surprise. "Do you carry that stuff on you at all times in case of a bondage emergency?"

"No." I cocked an eyebrow, rising to my feet. When I sat on the table next to her, she didn't flinch. Progress. "I brought this for you." I showed her my palm, feeling much like a magician about to do a trick for his audience. "Give me your hand." I slowly made two loops, twisted them inwards, and created a cuff with a pretty braid.

She held her breath as I slid it down her hand and onto her wrist. When I pulled in the tail end of the rope in the opposite direction, she automatically squeezed the smooth strands and let my fingers wrap around her wrist. The soft skin there prickled with goosebumps.

Caterina could be so alluring when she wasn't throwing insults at me or running away. Her breathing was even as she watched me gently pull, leading her toward me. I had never had to start this way with a rope bottom. It was way more satisfying than I thought it would be.

Say yes to me.

"Did that hurt?"

She glowered at me then blinked a few times. "No."

"Can you get out of it?"

She stripped the jute off her and sat back. "Yeah."

Her fingers released their hold on the rope and fell gently into mine. We had never held hands before. If she realized it, she didn't show it. We stayed like this—her bright, green gaze glued to mine, our bodies close, breathing the same air.

"Sign and then I'll answer all your questions," I whispered.

Her nipples perked up under the thin fabric of her dress, and she leaned into me. As usual, the spell never lasted very long with her. She shook her head as if to clear her thoughts and yanked her hand away from me.

"There." She quickly scribbled her name and shoved the paper toward me. "Let me see the contract. If you're trying to dissuade me from helping Dad, it's not going to work. I've made up my mind."

"I want this more than you know. But I need you to come to me with your eyes wide open." I reached behind me and grabbed her folder.

"Do all your submissives get a folder?"

"Rope bottoms. Yes."

She gasped. "That many?"

"I've been doing this for a long while. I like things to be in order."

"Did you have sex with all of them?" She asked casually while she opened the manila.

"How is that relevant to our arrangement?" A half-smile pulled at my lips.

"I guess it isn't." She shrugged, while her gaze stayed glued to the page. After a few beats, she shot to her feet. "I can't read while you're hovering over me with your broody stare." She glanced over at the grandfather clock by the entrance. "Omigod. How did it get to be this late? I have to get back to the hospital."

Shit. I had hoped to start tonight. Although, she would need more time to digest everything I had just thrown her way. I didn't like disappointment though. "Aaron will drive you. I expect an answer tomorrow."

"Tomorrow? Dad is in the hospital. I can't move all my stuff here and do what you want." The fear in her eyes dissipated and was replaced with determination. She was in her professional, get-it-done mode.

I could only hope that meant she was ready to agree to my terms. She raked a hand through her loose curls. Christ, I ached to bury my fingers in her hair, take in her scent, and kiss her. One more night. I could handle one more night without her.

"You will not need your things."

She furrowed her brows at me. "This is too much. I have to see Dad and then Google the heck out of this."

"I expected no less. You'll find everything you need in that folder."

She collected her papers and slowed down when she got to the photos. With a quick glance at me, she picked up those too and shoved them in her folder. *Good girl.* I walked behind her as she made her way to the double doors. The pressure in my chest grew with every step. As if I knew that if she left tonight, I would lose her forever.

I braced my hand on the wooden panel. When she spun around to glare at me, I caged her in. "If you and Michael leave the country, just know that there isn't a single corner on this Earth where you can hide from me."

Her cleavage rose and fell as she labored to catch her breath. The red in her cheeks was such a fucking turn on, I couldn't stand it anymore. I leaned in to take in her perfume and revel in her energy. When I made to step back, she jutted her chin upward.

"I see. So, this trust thing is a one-way deal. I need to surrender to you, but you can't even give me this small freedom of seeing Dad?" She pushed at my chest once, before sliding her hands down to my pecs.

Could she feel my heart racing underneath her palm? The awestruck look in her eyes told me she did. *We're done pretending, love. Aren't we?* I wracked my brain for a good reason why Caterina and I couldn't have this. Just this once. The plan was the plan. A kiss couldn't ruin that.

I pressed my thigh to her core. She rewarded me with a small sigh of pleasure and my name on her lips. "Rex." Her eyes fluttered closed. Caterina needed this as much as I did.

"You can go. But tomorrow I get my answer."

The look she gave me was of pure desire and raw need. A

hint of her scent sparked a flame below my navel. Suddenly, the room was too quiet, the air thick and hot, and my pulse out of control. Like water going fast down the drain, my restraint shot away from me—farther and farther, until I couldn't get it back.

Our gazes locked. She was so beautiful, and for once, she wasn't looking daggers at me. Oh, fuck it. I captured her mouth with mine, thrusting my tongue past her lips, while I cupped her cheek to keep her in place. All the pent-up frustration came gushing out of me in that kiss. All the times she told me she hated me, and all the times she recoiled from me. I took everything from her now, pressing my body to her soft flesh. Jesus, I ached to bury myself inside of her. She called for me again, rubbing her wet spot on my pants.

I could take her now, but where would that leave us? Me paying for sex? Her using her virginity to save her father? She had denied being a virgin before. But I knew the truth. I knew she had saved herself for someone good. That had been her mother's influence, and she'd been right. Someone like Caterina deserved so much more. She deserved a man who could give her all those things she wanted, like a home and a family. I wasn't that man. But I had other things to offer her.

I drank from her lips hungrily, even after I had decided I needed to stop. It took a few more minutes to give up on this fantasy, where Caterina had her arms around my neck, kissing me as if she had never been kissed before. I deepened the kiss and then pulled away. Her breath hitched from the abrupt change now that she no longer had my body supporting all of her weight against the door.

If she didn't have a reason to hate me before, she did now. The fire in her eyes told me she didn't get off. The frustration brought tears to her eyes. I shouldn't have done that. Our relationship was too fragile for this kind of added confusion.

"Aaron will drive you home so you can change out of that dress before you see Michael." I pointed at the wet spots all over her skirt.

I tried not to think of her pretty pussy all swollen for me, waiting. Instead, I imagined her going home and touching herself. A smirk pulled at my lips. For the first time ever, I knew without a shadow of a doubt that Caterina would be thinking of me the next time she climaxed.

"You're an asshole." She smoothed out the fabric. When she felt the moisture there, her cheeks turned a bright red. Pursing her lips, she turned on her heel and scrambled out of the room.

I took two strides and stopped before I made things worse. Before I sent it all to hell and fucked her into next week on the boardroom table. For Christ's sake, she had already said yes to that. I raked both hands through my hair and sauntered back to my chair.

Me: She's on her way. Take her home.

Aaron: She's in the car.

Me: Don't leave her side.

Aaron: Yes, sir.

I touched the faded white stain on my trousers and brought my fingers to my nose and mouth. *Tomorrow. We start tomorrow.*

CHAPTER 9
Letters of Bottoms Past

CATERINA

God, I hated him. I grabbed the bottle of water Aaron had left for me in the backseat beverage tray and chugged it. What exactly had happened? I went to Rex to ask for a favor and give him the one thing I thought he wanted, but then he refused me and counter-offered with something much, much worse than sex.

I glanced down at my dress. Heat rushed to my cheeks. Never in a million years would I have guessed Rex would have this effect on me. Everything he did tonight was a huge turn-on. How was that even possible? I had always thought he was attractive, well no, more like crazy hot with a devilish face that made him dangerous. I had never been touched like that before. My skin still burned in the places his strong hands had been.

And Jesus, that kiss!

In college, I fooled around plenty. Even if I never went all the way, I had gotten pretty close. I had kissed at least five guys. But none of them made me feel like Rex. He took control and devoured me. I shivered against the cool air. Now that I had several miles between us, my body temperature declined drastically.

I brought my fingers to my lips and let my head rest on the window. The memory of Rex sent more flutters to my pussy. They hadn't stopped since he wedged his thigh between my legs and pressed against my core. I had been so close to coming in front of him. What the hell was wrong with me? I drank more of the water and looked out just as Aaron pulled up to my building. I hadn't asked him to bring me here. No doubt he was following Rex's orders. I let it go because I did need to change before going back to the hospital to check in on Dad.

He should be done with all his tests by now. Hugging the folder close to my chest, I climbed out of the car as soon as we stopped and headed straight to my apartment, hoping I wouldn't run into any of my neighbors. They weren't noisy or anything, but I was just too frazzled right now to have a civilized conversation with another person.

I walked in the door and went straight to the shower to wash Rex's scent off of me and our entire interaction, really. After I got cleaned up, I dressed in a pair of jeans and T-shirt. When I sat down to put on my boots, I spotted the manila folder on the bed. My pulse quickened immediately. The contract was a thick document. I couldn't even begin to imagine what kind of terms Rex would have for me. Shit. I didn't have time for this. I had to see Dad. Rising to my feet, I grabbed my big purse and stuffed the papers inside it.

Aaron was on his phone when I walked up to him. He put it away immediately and did that thing where he moved quickly to let me in the car. Again, I didn't have to tell him where I was going. He knew I needed to see Dad.

"Thank you." I met his gaze in the rearview mirror.

"Just doing my job." He dipped his head.

At the hospital, Aaron dropped me off at the front entrance where Nurse Sam came out to greet me. If this was Rex's way of smoothing things over with me, I supposed it was working. I was a ball of nerves waiting to hear about Dad's tests and surgery.

"Ms. Alfera, I was told you were on your way here. Mr. Alfera is awake. His tests are in good shape. He's scheduled for surgery first thing in the morning." He ushered me down the hallway to the elevator bay.

I counted at least five of Rex's guys along the way. They were by the main lobby, the elevators, the nurses' station, and two near Dad's room. When we were kids, Dad insisted we keep a security detail. Overtime, he got used to the idea of being a regular citizen and gave up on the strict precautions. Now that he was under Rex's protection, it seemed the bodyguards were needed again.

"Thank you. Would I be able to stay with him?" I asked Nurse Sam when he opened the door to Dad's private room.

"Of course. I'll get you some blankets and a pillow." He smiled and left the way we had come.

Dad's room smelled of disinfectant and new plastic. But for a hospital room, it was nice. The large windows at the far end let in plenty of light and offered a great view of the city. Seeing Dad like this broke my heart, and it also scared the shit out of me. I couldn't lose him too. I ambled over to his bed. As soon as I placed a hand on his blanketed foot, he opened his eyes.

"Hey, Bells. I was hoping you'd stay home for tonight." He patted my hand.

"I can't do that knowing you're here."

"Such a fuss. These doctors ought to know you can't mend a broken heart." He gestured to the machines hooked up to his arm. "You don't need to worry about me."

"I'm doing it anyway." I gave him what I hoped was a happy smile. My heart hurt for him. "So big day tomorrow?"

"I suppose." He shrugged. "I'm tired. Maybe if they stopped prodding and let me sleep, I would get better faster."

"Did you eat?"

"I did." He deadpanned.

"Want to watch TV?"

"That sounds nice." The sadness in his eyes was unbearable.

I knew what he wanted to say—that he didn't need heart surgery. He needed Mom back. Blinking away tears, I busied myself with the remote. I scrolled through the guide until I found a documentary on lions living in sub-Saharan Africa. Within minutes, Dad's breathing settled into an even rhythm. His weak heart had to do with how tired he felt. Until his surgery, there wasn't much else the doctors could do to help him.

Nurse Sam returned with a set of pillows and a blue blanket, and then gave me a quick rundown of what to expect in the morning. When he left, I settled into the oversized lazy boy near the window. I propped my bag on the side of the chair and stopped with my hand hovering over the contract.

I thought of Rex and all the photos he had shown me. Photos I had brought with me. Blood rushed through me as my head snapped up to Dad. He was fast asleep with his face tilted away from me. Somehow that felt like I had a bit of privacy.

Letting out a long breath, I reached for the folder and set it on my lap. I flipped through the pages without really reading anything in particular. When I got to the end, I noticed a set of handwritten notes. The cover page had Rex's letterhead. I rubbed my clammy hands on my pants and picked the letter. His tone was business like and polite, which made me wonder if these were his own words. In real life, he was dourer and demanding.

I focused on the last paragraph.

Caterina,

You can do your own research on kinbaku or shibari, but you won't find what you're looking for. Which is why I have included three testimonials from women who have partnered with me. They know about you and have graciously volunteered to answer all your questions. I do hope you take them up on their offer.

Rex

Was he fucking kidding me? His contract included letters of bottoms past? I supposed he wasn't all that wrong. I didn't need to know where kinbaku came from or what it entailed. I needed to hear from women who had done it. More specifically, I wanted to know what kind of Dom Rex was. Was he cruel? Was he rough and impatient like his kiss had been? I squirmed in my seat at the thought that maybe our sessions might include more kisses like that.

I shook my head to clear my thoughts and opened the first note, furrowing my brows at her bubbly tone. Violet was excited I had decided to take Rex up on his offer. She assured me she had tried to get back on his schedule for the past two years and hadn't had any luck. I rolled my eyes every time she called me a lucky girl. I stopped counting at five. Violet had a few tips on floor exercises to do to stay flexible and promote body awareness. What the fuck? She ended her testimonial by offering one last piece of advice.

Enjoy your time. But whatever you do, don't fall for him. You'll be alone in that effort. Rex's heart doesn't work that way.

Lucky for me, I already hated the guy. My problem would be not scratching his eyes out during one of our bondage sessions. I dropped my head in my hands. Thanks to Rex, bondage session was now in my vocabulary. I hated him all right. I threw the covers aside and ambled toward the body-guard outside. Aaron had also joined the crew. He wasn't here for Dad. He was here for me. Jeez whatever for? To make sure I didn't leave the country?

"Could you put his number in my phone?" I gave him my mobile.

"Of course." He didn't even ask whose number I wanted. Everything in our world revolved around Rex.

"Thanks." I turned around and returned to my makeshift bed. My heart raced a little knowing I had Rex's number now.

I thought about what I would say to him. More like, I fantasized about calling him to tell him the whole thing was off. That I would find another way to get him his money. But all the scenarios that played in my head were nothing more than a pretend world where I called the shots instead of Rex. I glared at the screen, my forefinger hovering over his name, while I imagined him sitting at the head of the table in the boardroom with his ankle braced on his knee. After several minutes, I closed my eyes. When his impossibly beautiful face appeared in my mind's eye, I didn't chase it away. I hugged the contract to my chest along with my phone and let myself drift off to sleep.

The next morning, my day started with a whirlwind of nurses and doctors taking Dad away for his surgery. Nurse Sam promised to give me updates via text and recommended I go home since the surgery and recovery would take hours. Numb, I did as he asked. But after several minutes of pacing up and down my apartment, I decided to go to work instead. I needed the distraction, not to mention, I had several projects pending that required my attention.

I hopped in the shower and donned a pant suit in a peachy color. The outfit had the desired effect of making me feel like I was in control of my life. Of course, some of that went away when I met up with Aaron outside my building, and he promptly informed me he had orders to stay with me all day. I opened my mouth to tell him I didn't need a babysitter, but then decided it would be easier just to let him tag along.

"Hey, Cat." Sarah knitted her brows from behind her desk when she saw me outside her office.

"Hey." I leaned on the doorframe.

"How's your dad? What are you doing here?"

"He's in surgery right now. I was going crazy at my place waiting for news."

"Well, I'm not gonna send you home. We need the help." She pointed toward the set of cubicles in the middle of the floor and the commotion of voices, phones ringing, and keyboards clicking. "Some big wig investor is coming over to see how we're doing. The boss is beside herself trying to get statuses on all projects and financials."

"I better get to work then." I waved and headed to my office at the end of the hall.

I sat on my chair and fired up my computer. This normalcy was exactly what I needed today. I smoothed out the soft fabric of my trousers, and Rex's voice echoed in my mind. "You will not need your things." What had he meant by that? I stole a quick glance to the chaos outside my door then grabbed Rex's contract from my purse.

Flipping through the pages, I got to the section titled: Living Arrangements. He expected me to live in his penthouse, wear the clothes he would choose for me every day, and basically be his pet. Why would anyone with a choice want to do this? Pursing my lips, I grabbed a red pen and started crossing out items I didn't agree with. I wasn't going to let Rex bully me into any of this crap.

Suddenly, the air shifted in the room. Out on the floor, the staff members had stopped their chattering and typing. I walked around my desk to see what had happened. When Rex turned the corner at the end of the hallway, adrenaline shot through me. He took long, confident strides across the way and headed straight for my boss's corner office. What the hell was he doing here? I hid behind my door, while my heart thrashed in my ears.

"Hello?" Sarah rapped on the window.

"Yeah." My body jerked in surprise. Maybe I had imagined the whole thing. I took in a breath and opened the door. "What's going on?"

"Did you see the email? Impromptu meeting in five."

"No, I didn't see it." I checked my watch. Apparently, I had spent the last two hours revising Rex's contract. "I wonder what this is about." I grabbed my iPad and motioned for her to lead the way.

"It's probably about that big wig I told you about."

Our company leased the entire tenth floor, but we shared conference room space with other tenants two floors up. To get to the elevator bay, we had to walk by the corner office. I stole a few glances at him while Sarah pressed the call button a few times. From where I stood, I could only see the back of the man in there. But it was definitely Rex.

"Are you coming?" Sarah waved a hand in front of me to get my attention.

"What? I mean yes." I hopped on the car and the doors slid closed.

As soon as we started moving, I relaxed against the mirrored wall. Rex just had a way to put me on edge. What the hell was he doing here? He couldn't possibly be expecting me to go with him today. I had barely finished going through the entirety of the document he wanted me to sign. And I had a ton of changes he needed to make.

I followed Sarah into the conference room and found a seat at the far end of the table. When I looked up, I met Rex's gaze on the other side of the glass wall. He was with my boss, who was practically sprinting to keep up with his pace while she talked with exaggerated hand gestures. Wait, what? This was his meeting?

CHAPTER 10
Can't Stand the Wait

CATERINA

"Jesus fuck." Sarah gripped my forearm and leaned in toward me to mouth. "Is that the Adonis from the hospital?"

"I don't know." I shrugged. "Is he?"

Sarah squinted at me in disbelief. As if anyone could meet Rex and then forget about him, his face, or the raw charge that trailed behind him wherever he went. As soon as he sauntered in, a stillness spread across the conference room table. Rex's gaze cut away from me as he went to stand at the front of the room. I tried really hard not to roll my eyes at that. He couldn't barge in and start acting like he owned A-List or this building. In spite of what he believed; he wasn't the king of everything.

He seemed so out of place here surrounded by cheap office furniture and bad overhead lighting. Rex Valentino was the king of a century old underground criminal society. Power and money had been part of his upbringing. He had been groomed to rule. Thinking of him perched on his high-back leather chair, next to old books, mahogany, and whiskey made more sense than this stuffy conference room.

My boss, Jill, joined him with a nervous smile and apologetic eyes, as if asking him for permission to be that close to him or to take over the meeting.

"Thank you everyone for joining us on such short notice. Mr. Valentino is here to learn more about our firm and see how we do things. So, he'll be sitting in on our weekly status meeting today. Which I realize is a day early." She put up her hand when other staff members exchanged concerned glances.

Rex shifted his weight and stuffed his hands in his trousers. Next to me, Sarah squeezed her legs together and let out a little sigh. I couldn't blame her. Rex in a dark-tailored suit was an aphrodisiac. I quickly scanned the room. Everyone was more or less in the same trance, even the men. Could they sense it? Did they know what Rex was? A ruthless mobster.

When I turned my attention back to Rex, his intense gaze zeroed in on me. A spark fluttered in my belly right before my imagination flashed a series of warped memories—a mix of the events from last night and the fantasies he planted in my head. I should be afraid. Where the hell was my sense of self-preservation?

"Pretend I'm not here." A half-smirk pulled at his lips, then he motioned for Jill to go on with the meeting.

Had he meant that for me? A little inside joke? Ignoring him had been so much easier before he kissed me, before he almost made me come with just the brush of his thigh.

I busied myself with my notes while he stared at me. I didn't have to look up to know he was doing exactly that. He was here to intimidate me and torture me like always.

Except, this time, he had gone too far. When he played the

part of predator in his own mafia world, it was like it was contained in the pages of a dark fairytale book. But here? At my work, my world? I realized he was very real and so was his offer to make me his rope bottom—for the small price of one million dollars. To me, it was way more than that. This arrangement between us was to save Dad.

I glanced up and met his gaze. He didn't look away. He didn't smile either. He simply stared at me as if he owned me, as if he wanted to remind me of that fact. The contract waiting downstairs in my office was merely a formality, our terms of engagement. But the part where my body and soul now belonged to him—that was sealed the minute I stumbled into his boardroom.

Jill did her best to conduct our status meeting like she would any other day—mafia king aside. I managed to keep it together until she called on me to report on the campaigns I was working on and also the new clients I had been courting. Next to her, Rex knitted his brows. Why? In disbelief? What did he think I did for a living? Got Jill coffee and donuts?

Slowly, I rose to my feet and tapped on my iPad to bring up the numbers I had put together last week. I didn't care what Rex thought of me—if he thought I was smart or capable. None of it mattered, not for what he wanted me for.

"Go on, Cat." Jill motioned for me to start.

"Thank you." I looked away from him and focused on my boss instead. Over the years, I had gotten really good at pretending he didn't exist. His kiss burned on my lips, but I quickly wiped it off with the back of my hand and moved on to the task at hand. My top three projects were ahead of schedule, which put a big smile on Jill's face. "On the new accounts, I met with Mr. Suede, and he's agreed to let us take a stab at his new campaign. As far as Mr. Ricci, I've yet to get a hold of him. I know he's been meeting with other agencies. I just need to get him on the phone."

"Thomas?" Rex asked and suddenly the temperature in the room shot up to a million degrees. "Thomas Ricci is a good friend. I can get you a meeting."

"I don't think that's necessary," I fired back.

"Cat." Jill's gaze darted between me and Rex.

"Anyway, that's all I have. Thanks." I sat, looking daggers at him, while hot blood rushed through me. He had no right to come here and interfere.

"Let me know if you change your mind." He flashed me a smile that made Sarah squeak next to me.

As soon as Jill ended the meeting, I shot to my feet and scurried out of there. I needed the safety of my office, where Rex couldn't get to me. Sarah caught up to me near the elevators. She rushed in front of me and hit the call button.

"My ovaries are shot." She stepped into the car and leaned on the mirror wall. "I think I'm pregnant."

Across the way, through the glass wall, Rex stood in the middle of the conference room talking to Jill. Right before the doors slid closed, his gaze cut to me. My breath hitched, and I stepped back, closer to Sarah.

"Do you think we'll see more of Rex if he decides to invest? I wouldn't mind the daily dose of eye candy." Sarah held onto the rail as the old elevator clanked and whined on its way down.

"No idea. I'll see you later, okay?" I hugged my iPad and stepped out.

"Yeah, bye."

I shut my office door and leaned against it. Why did I let

him get to me? My heart pumped hard for at least another minute before it settled into a normal rhythm. Aahh! I fisted my hands and walked around my desk to get back to work. My first order of business would be to get a meeting scheduled with Mr. Ricci. That account would be a huge win for the agency. But I wanted to do it without Rex's help. I already owed him too much. What would he ask of me in return for that small favor? I shivered at the idea that Rex would want more from me apart from my complete surrender. What else was there for me to give to him?

"That was a good meeting." His voice startled me back to reality.

Rex Valentino in my office space was a new kind of torture.

"What do you want, Rex?" I glowered at him. "I didn't think you ever left your lair."

He glanced up, as if asking the heavens for patience. Then with two long strides, he reached for my door, shut it, then locked it. We were alone. If I screamed, would anyone come to help me?

"You know what I want." He let the blinds fall over the only window in the room, then turned to face me.

My gaze fell to the folder sitting on my desk. He followed the line of sight and smirked. "Ah. There it is."

He took the chair across from me, undoing his jacket before he reached for the contract. "Do you have any questions?" His eyebrows shot up in surprise when he flipped through the red-inked pages. I was sure at some point he smiled at the small devil I had drawn on the corner of the page and labeled Rex. "A month?" He raised an eyebrow.

He meant the section where it stated that our arrangement

would be for a year. A whole fucking year. "I can't pause my life for longer than that. I have twenty days of vacation time. That's all I can give you."

"That's nowhere near enough time to cover Michael's debt. Six months."

"Three."

"Six." He braced his arms on his knees. "May I remind you that you have no leverage here?"

"I can't take that much time off."

"Jill is very supportive of her staff working from home. For as long as the agency is still hers anyway." He scratched the stubble on his jaw.

Jill? He said her name with such familiarity, I had to wonder if they knew each other from before. Did they? I shook my head to stay focused on the second part of his statement. *"For as long as the agency is still hers"* sounded like our days in this office were numbered.

"What is that supposed to mean? Wait. Are you buying A-List? Why? What do you want with an advertising firm?"

"It's good business."

"Since when are you in the advertising business? What exactly are you planning to do with us?"

Rex's bread and butter was crime. It was how the Society had amassed billions in the last hundred years. Whatever Rex was thinking, it had to be illegal. Or at the very least, not good for the company. What would he do? Take it apart and sell it by the pound? Because that was the only way for him to make money off of us. He couldn't do this to me.

"Don't do this."

"I'm not running a charity, love. Don't tell me how to run my own company." His hard stern tone told me how serious he was about this transaction and how little he cared about my opinion or my feelings.

"You're despicable. You stood in our meeting for an hour, looked everyone in the eye, knowing you were here to destroy their livelihoods. Don't you have a heart?"

"No, I don't. I thought we had already established that." He turned his attention back to the contract. "The living arrangements are non-negotiable. You will live with me for the duration of the contract, and you will wear what I decide."

I blinked fast, unable to meet his dark gaze. This wasn't the Rex who had kissed me in the boardroom. The man sitting in front of me was the cruel mobster I knew him to be. He was here to collect on Dad's debt in the form of that contract. I had been naive to think I had a say in what our agreement would look like.

"I do need time to make sure Dad is okay. He can't be alone all that time."

"He won't be. I've arranged for a nurse to go home with him. He will be taken care of. I promise you that." He said it all while still reviewing my changes. "The body awareness sessions are for your benefit. Without them, you could get hurt. You will do them." He slow-blinked, and then blew out a breath. Was he trying to be patient with me? "Caterina, this contract is for your own good. It's what other bottoms have agreed to because it works. As your rigger, my job is to do anything in my power to ensure you're safe." His tone had a different quality to it, somehow kinder and under-standing.

"I don't know what half of that stuff is." I pointed at the pages in his hands. "What the hell is a reverse shrimp? And gagging? Hair binding? How is that even a thing?"

"Gyaku Ebi." He pronounced the words I had left out perfectly. "I will teach you."

"Those letters from your previous clients? That was a farce. I'd like to read the one-star raters." I crossed my arms over my chest.

Amusement registered in his eyes. "You just have to trust me."

"And you decided the best way to earn my trust is to tear apart the company I work for."

"Those two things are mutually exclusive."

"What? How? This is my job. You're taking it away just because you want me to be your pet." I hated how he made my voice tremble so much when he was around.

"Pet is the wrong term." He sat back calmly. We were in my office and still, he looked like he owned this place, like he owned me. "This practice will be more enlightening if you don't fight it. Don't fight me on this, love." His eyes softened along with his features. He felt familiar when he did that— when he regarded me as if we were complicit, partners in crime, equals. "I can't stand the wait."

A ribbon of desire swirled in my core. This version of Rex was so much harder to repudiate. Did he know that? Did he know how he affected me when he wasn't being a complete asshole? He had to know.

"Have dinner with me tonight." It wasn't a question.

"My father is in surgery as we speak. I don't have time for dates."

"It's not a date. It's a business meeting." He tossed the contract on my desk. "To finalize our terms. You will sign the agreement tonight." When I didn't move, he cleared his throat and nodded once. "Aaron will take you to see Michael. Dinner is at eight. My place."

"Don't you get tired of bossing people around?" I stood and braced my hands on my desk.

Slowly, he rose to his feet while he swept his gaze over my body. Heat rushed to my cheeks as images of his kiss flooded my mind. Also, I couldn't help but be painfully aware that he had seen me naked. And more than that, he had almost seen me come. My nipples hardened at the memory of Rex's suit rubbing against my chest.

He leaned forward until his face was inches from mine. "No, I don't. I'm very much looking forward to the day when you do exactly as I say." His warm breath brushed my face. He smelled so good, a mix of mahogany and Rex's signature musk. "Eight o'clock. Wear the dress."

"What dress?" I furrowed my brows in confusion.

He glanced down at his phone with a satisfied smirk then braced his palms on my desk. "The one being delivered to your apartment as we speak."

He reached for my chin, and I jerked my head away from him. His smile faded some, and that gave me a surge of satisfaction. I hadn't exactly won this round, but anything that wiped that infuriating smirk off his face was a win for me. Though something told me he would make me pay for it later.

CHAPTER 11
Leave It to Me

Rex

"Home, sir?" Frank, my driver and bodyguard, met my gaze in the rearview mirror.

"No, I just got a text from Michael's nurse. He's awake."

"Yes, sir." He put the car in gear and peeled off the curb to merge into the incoming traffic.

I settled into the back seat of my SUV and worked on getting my breath under control. When it came to Caterina, nothing was ever straight forward, nothing ever went the way I wanted it to, and I was losing patience. Though I could see she had come to terms with the fact that there was no way out for her. If she wanted to keep her dad out of jail, she would have to say yes to me.

My hand pressed on the manila folder. Smiling, I flipped through the pages layered in red ink. She had read every single clause and had countered with something different, which meant she was willing to make this work. I had hoped she would stay home with me tonight, but she needed more time. I had already waited two years for this, I could wait another day or so.

At the hospital, I entered through a private entrance in the parking garage and took the elevator to the third floor. Something felt off. But no one could be stupid enough to mount an attack on the Society in broad daylight and in a public building. As I made my way down the sterile corridor, the hair at the nape of my neck prickled, and I couldn't ignore my instincts any longer. I reached inside my jacket, flipped the safety strap on my shoulder holster and wrapped my fingers around the grip of my nine-millimeter.

When I turned the corner at the end of the hallway, I found three of my men unconscious on the floor. I rushed to them and checked their pulses. Joey and Mike were still alive. Marco was dead. Mother fucker. Who had the guts to come to a crowded place and do this to us? I got on my phone and called Frank, who picked up on the first ring.

"Get a cleaning crew in here."

"Jesus Christ. Right away."

Tossing my phone in my pocket, I darted toward Michael's room. My heart pumped hard and fast. The steady rhythm cleared my thoughts and allowed me to focus on what I had to do next. I pulled out my gun and pressed my back against the wall. While I listened for any movement inside the room, I threaded a silencer onto the barrel. Then I peeked inside. Sure as fuck, there was a man there shoving a pillow over Michael's face with his back to me. I exhaled and stepped into his line of sight. A single shot was all I allowed myself. We were in a hospital for Christ's sake.

I got him in the knee cap. *Dead men don't tell tales.* He spun around with a confused look on his face. His gaze darted from his knee and up to me as if he couldn't figure out what had happened to him. The shock of being in pain wore off and he limped to the edge of the bed. I had him cornered. If he wanted to leave the room, he'd have to go through me.

"Do you know who this is?" I jerked my chin toward Michael, who seemed to be unconscious.

"A fucking criminal," the man spat.

"Who sent you?"

The man swayed and put his hands up in the air. He hadn't lost so much blood that he'd be dizzy. I furrowed my brows and aimed my firearm at him again as he stepped back toward the open window. In the next breath, while I finally realized what he was about to do, he let himself drop. I rushed toward him, but it was too late. No way he could survive a three-story fall. I squinted and searched for him on the rooftop below me, but he was gone. Jumping out the window had been his exit strategy. This man wasn't some random asshole. *He was a professional.*

After I made sure we were alone, I hit the call button for the nurses' station. Sam darted into the room, his eyes wide in surprise.

"What the hell?" He frowned at the splattered blood on the floor, while he checked Michael's vitals and placed an oxygen mask over his mouth.

"I know. This was a gutsy move." I unscrewed the silencer and holstered my gun.

Sam was one of ours. In our line of work, having a medical professional with access to a hospital was an invaluable asset. He was the best we had, which was why he had been assigned to take care of Caterina's dad.

"Is he okay?" My chest tightened at the idea of having to

tell Caterina that her dad was killed. That would be on me if that happened.

"Yeah, the old man is tougher than we all think."

"Don't let the wrinkles on my face fool you, I'm not that easy to kill." Michael pulled the mask off and coughed. I chose not to mention that, when I walked in, Michael had not tried to fight back. He hadn't moved at all. His gaze bore into mine for a long minute before he conceded with a nod. "You saved my life. Why?"

"We're family. I need you alive."

"Is the throne giving you hemorrhoids already?" He chuckled at his own joke.

There was a time when his smoker's voice terrified me. There was a time when I looked up to him like an uncle. But that was before he abdicated, before he left the Society for good. Michael was a coward who didn't deserve his daughter's sacrifice.

"You would know, wouldn't you?" I stuffed my hands in my pockets. "Once again, you owe Caterina your life." That got me the desired reaction. His murky eyes watered, and he squeezed them tight. He had lost his wife and was about to lose his only daughter. "That asshole trying to kill you was a professional."

"Hired guns don't use pillows." Sam replaced Michael's saline bag then examined the needles in his hand.

"They do if they're trying to hide what they are." I met Michael's gaze. "The question is, is that asshole trying to kill Michael Alfera over old grievances, or was he simply going after a member of the Society."

"The latter." Michael placed a hand on his forehead.

The fear that registered in his eyes sent a shock of adrenaline through me. If someone out there had orders to execute our members, that meant we were all at risk, that our identity had been discovered. If whoever this asshole was knew about Michael, he knew about Massimo, Enzo...and Caterina.

"Now you see Dad was right. The Society is under attack. Someone knows we're still here. And they're hell bent on eliminating us one by one."

The motives could be anything—revenge, money, someone wanted to take over the Society, or they just wanted us gone.

"I didn't think that was possible," Michael croaked.

"Sam, give us a minute." I motioned for Sam to leave the room.

With a nod, he quickly made his way out and shut the door behind him. Last night, I had called for an extraordinary assembly of all members of the Society because the families needed a truce. We needed to join our resources and go after the son of a bitch who killed the Gallos and Dad. If Michael had sided with me, they all would've fallen in line. I needed to make them understand the threat was real.

"Did he say anything to you?" I pointed toward the window, a reference to his would-be killer.

"The usual." He snorted. "That I was going to die like the pig I am." He squinted at the wall, as if trying to recall the details of the assault. "Maybe, I saw a badge inside his jacket. I don't know. You know in all my years in the mob, there was only one group of people concerned with pigs and how they die."

"The cops."

He shook his forefinger at me. "More specifically, FBI."

"You have proof? The badge could've been fake." I

stepped toward him. For the first time since Dad died, I felt like I was making progress on the promise I made to him.

"Maybe."

"What else did he say?"

"Nothing more. He wasn't after revenge. I can tell you that much." He placed the oxygen mask over his mouth. After a few breaths, he went on. "In my time, I had to take care of many fathers, mothers, sisters, brothers. Every time, their family members would come for me with a shaky pistol in their hands and hatred in their eyes. They could never just shoot me. They wanted me to know why I was dying by their hand. They'd give me a whole sob story about who their loved ones were, what they meant to them, how I robbed them of someone they cared for." His voice trailed off as he struggled to inhale.

I stepped toward him and helped him with the mask. His eyes cut to me as if asking, "do you get my meaning?" A smirk played on his lips as if he found the irony of it all amusing. The old man truly believed he was hard to kill. Maybe he was right. The real irony was that Michael had lost the will to live, and yet he lived on. He had survived long enough to know the pain of losing someone he loved. For all his money and power, he couldn't save his wife.

"He called you a fucking criminal. If this isn't about revenge, then that only leaves duty. The asshole who tried to kill you is a fed? A fucking uniform?" I chuckled, rubbing the stubble on my face. "A pig."

"Find my sons," Michael begged.

Seeing him like this, defeated and alone, made my stomach churn. He had selfishly turned our world upside down to be with Caterina's mom. And for what? Nothing he did changed anything. He and his entire family were back in the thick of it.

As it always played out, an innocent like Caterina would have to pay for Michael's mistakes.

"Please."

"I already know where they are. It's time they come home."

"Yes, it is." The old man sighed in relief. "And Caterina?"

"Thanks to you. She's mine to keep."

"Her brothers won't stand for it." He glowered at me. "She doesn't deserve this. She's good."

"It's not up to them. Just like it's not up to you anymore."

The old man was right. Caterina was good. But our enemies didn't care who or what she was. They intended to destroy our way of life and she was a huge part of that equation. She was mine to protect. "She'll be safe with me. You trusted my father once with the reins of the Society. I need you to trust me now."

Almost thirty years ago, Michael Alfera fell in love with an artist. He lost all reason and sense of allegiance. He was the king of everything, but for his wife Anna, he chose to leave the Society and leave Dad in charge. A decision that eventually put me on my current path. I had never wanted to be king. But duty came first. It was high time Michael remembered that.

He nodded. "What do you need?"

"Call Signoria Vittoria and tell her this truce needs to happen. If the families don't fall in line, we won't survive this thing coming for us."

"And in return, you'll keep my family safe?"

"You have my word." I offered him my hand.

He glared at it for a several breaths and then accepted it with a weak shake. "What happens now? Your father and I made a lot of enemies in the eighties. The FBI has been at our heels since forever. And sure, they have so much red tape to go through, they can't get to us. That has played in our favor for decades. But don't make the mistake of underestimating them. That's not how you stay alive."

"Leave it to me."

Frank caught up with me outside Michael's room. "It's all taken care of. We lost Marco." He pursed his lips. "Those sons of bitches can't keep doing this to us."

"Agreed."

"What do we do, boss?"

"Have you heard from Aaron?" A ribbon of adrenaline fluttered in my stomach. Who knew how determined the asshole who tried to off Michael was? Did he go after Caterina as soon as he jumped out the window? I had no doubt he had survived the fall.

"Not yet. I've tried a few times. Should I go to Ms. Alfera's home?"

"No. I got it. I need you to stay on this asshole's trail—see if anyone checks in at a hospital or clinic with a broken leg or a shot to the knee or both." I squeezed Frank's shoulder. "He won't get away with it. You have my word."

"You can't go alone."

"I won't." I pointed at two of my guys. "You're with me." Then I turned to Frank. "I need Michael alive. Get more men in here. Get a whole fucking army if you need to."

"Yes, sir."

I strode out of the hospital with my men close behind me. My hand rested on the gun holstered inside my suit jacket. Caterina had stayed in her office after I left her. Aaron was with her, but if he hadn't touched base with us, it was because something had gone wrong. I stopped at the entrance to the hospital and waited for my guys to do their checks. When they nodded, I darted to the SUV and climbed in the backseat.

"We're going back to Madison to pick up Caterina." I fished my mobile out of my pocket and called Aaron. My pulse spiked as I waited ring after ring. When he didn't answer, I uttered a string of profanities then left him a message to warn him.

"Floor it. He's not picking up."

Michael had warned me not to underestimate the FBI. Well, the uniforms had made that mistake today. This attack on Michael in broad daylight, while he was still at the hospital, was a direct insult to me. It said they thought I would stand back and let them fuck us over.

Two good things had come out of this incident with the alleged feds, though. One, I had an idea of who was after the Society. And two, I had made up my mind about my arrangement with Caterina.

Before, I was willing to go at the pace she needed because I knew it was all too much to digest in one night, because I knew she was worried about her father. But now that her life was at risk and she needed me, I couldn't wait any longer. Caterina wasn't leaving my high-rise after tonight.

CHAPTER 12
Tie Me Up, Tie Me Down

REX

Red spots clouded my vision as my driver ran the light to get ahead of traffic. The fast beating of my heart had turned into an odd buzzing in my head, like the bombinating of a thousand bees. I didn't mind the pain in my chest. It gave me focus. All I could wish for was that this ache wouldn't be permanent. When I lost Mom, I went to a very dark place, a state of mind that I never thought I'd recover from until I began studying kinbaku.

My driver weaved through traffic in a chaos of screeching tires and honking horns. When we rounded the corner and her building came into view, I swallowed hard and focused on getting control of my breathing again. If the FBI went after Caterina tonight, I would have no choice but to retaliate in a way they had never seen before.

The Society had gone underground shortly after the Great Depression. The families found that dealing in secrecy was much more efficient than having to butt heads with the feds at every turn. Every now and then, the FBI would come close to uncovering who we were and how we operated. But all those times, after they spun their wheels and exhausted their resources, they got nothing but smoke.

As far as loyalties went, I didn't trust Michael one bit. Back when he ran the Society, everything he did was to serve himself. I didn't give a fuck if he now considered himself reformed, simply because he found love and got himself a family. He acted like he was the first man to ever earn all that bliss.

I would be an idiot if I didn't take his warning seriously, though. He had no proof the uniforms were after us. In my world, everyone was guilty until proven otherwise. No way in hell was this happening on my watch. I wasn't about to let the pigs kill us all off one by one.

"Keep the car running." I tapped my driver on the shoulder and then turned to my other guy. "Check the perimeter."

I darted to the front entrance. By some miracle, the doors to the elevator car slid open as soon as I reached it. I hopped on and hit the call button for Caterina's floor. For the second time today, I unholstered my firearm, but kept it hidden inside my suit jacket in case I ran into one of Caterina's neighbors. Civilians had a thing about calling the cops whenever they were spooked. If I thought the cops could handle this matter for us, I would've called them myself.

After what felt like an eternity of hotel lobby music, the car stopped. I inhaled, and in the next breath, I stepped out and silently made my way to Caterina's door. Her furious voice filtered through the walls in a whirling of furniture getting knocked over and muffled whimpers. I didn't allow myself time to check in with my guy. This was Caterina in danger. I had to save her.

I gripped my gun and barged in. My body temperature went from cold to hot as I ambled toward Caterina holding a butcher's knife to Aaron's throat.

"What the hell is going on?" I slammed the door shut. The apartment shook, and I winced. So much for keeping her neighbors out of this.

"Are you kidding me right now?" She shot me a glare that actually made me step back. "There's a fucking stranger in my home. A stranger that you—" she waved the blade in my direction, which gave Aaron the opportunity to get away from her, "—sent to spy on me. I'm the one who should be asking what the hell is going on in that thick head of yours?"

I inhaled and held my breath until my brain processed the fact that Caterina was safe. Pissed off as all fuck, but alive and well. With all the patience I could muster, because I knew this misunderstanding had not been his fault, I holstered my gun and shifted my gaze toward Aaron. "We called and you didn't answer. You know the rules."

His cheeks and ears turned red. If he was angry or embarrassed, I couldn't tell. I would be both if a woman had bested me the way Caterina had fought him off. He had been trained to handle any kind of situation. "She tossed my phone out the window."

"Why?" I pinched my nose.

"I wanted him out of my apartment." She braced her hands on her hips, and my hand itched for a bit of rope.

"I got the message about the clean-up crew. I figured it would be safer if I kept my eyes on her."

"While I got dressed?"

"I wasn't going to look." Aaron's eyes went wide in panic. He knew what Caterina meant to me. He knew what the punishment would be if he so much as touched her.

I put my hand up to get him to stop. "I understand. Did you clear the apartment?"

"Yes, sir."

"You did the right thing. Go find your goddamn phone." I gestured toward the door. When it shut behind him, I turned my attention to Caterina. Her cheeks were flushed while she stood at the ready with a big ass knife in her hand. With my hands up in surrender, I stalked toward her. "I get that you don't trust me, but you put yourself in danger today with your antics."

"I get that you think you own me because of my dad's debt, but you don't. And you don't get to send random guys to barge into my home. Come to think of it, you don't get to barge in either." She raised her arm higher as if aiming for my face, rather than my gut.

"Jesus fuck. We don't have time for this." The bombinating in my head returned and all I could think of was getting her to a safe place. I closed the space between us, grabbed her wrist and squeezed it until she let go with a whimper. "Your life is in danger. We need to go."

"Get out of my house. Our dinner is off." She shoved at my chest. "You think everyone is after you."

"That's because they are." I bent down, wrapped my arm around the back of her legs and hoisted her over my shoulder.

"Have you lost your mind?" She fisted my suit jacket.

When she realized she had access to my weapon, her body twisted as her hands roamed my back.

If she weren't trying to shoot me, I would've enjoyed her touch. "Don't even think about it." I darted toward the elevators. The digital screen on the side panel showed it was two floors down.

"Then put me down." She went limp on my shoulder, then started screaming and kicking. "Help."

I set her down and clamped my hand over her mouth. My phone vibrated with a message, and just because this night had gone all wrong, I knew it wasn't good news. "I need to get that," I whispered in her ear. "If you run or scream again, our deal is off."

She stiffened in my arms, then nodded. As soon as she did, I fished my phone out of my pocket. "Son of a bitch."

"Having a bad day?" She smirked.

"No, love. You're having a bad day. I'm trying to fucking help you." I grabbed her arm, possibly a little harder than needed, and headed for the stairwell. Aaron had found one of my guys knocked out in the courtyard behind her building. That could only mean one thing. The feds had come for her too. While we rushed to the garage level, I called Aaron. "Where are you?"

"Courtyard. The two men went inside. It's safe to come out."

"Got it. We'll meet you there." I hung up and turned to Caterina, who had finally realized this wasn't a game. "What's the best way to get to the back entrance?"

"Through the garage. There's an access door on the far end."

"Go." I motioned for her to lead.

The terror in her eyes told me she had a million questions running through her mind. But she knew she needed to get to safety now and figure out the rest later. She picked up the pace, holding on to the rail for balance until she reached the bottom floor. Gasping for air, she pushed the door and pointed toward the other end.

I nodded and took the lead from there. Shielding her with my body, I ushered her toward the back. We came up to an alley that smelled of trash and had a few cars parked to the side. That was a good thing because that meant Aaron had a way to get to us.

In the next beat, my SUV turned the corner with wheels screeching. Who knew if Caterina ever had any kind of training, but even now that she knew she was in danger, she remained calm, and to my satisfaction, she obeyed my orders.

"Get in." I opened the door when the car jerked to a stop in front of us. She did as I asked and even made room for me in the backseat. "Go." I tapped Aaron's shoulder. "Where are the others?"

"I put them in a taxi. They're on their way to the Crucible."

"Good." I sat back and released a breath before I reached for Caterina's cold hand. "Are you okay?"

"Yeah." She pulled away from me as if my touch repulsed her.

I swallowed the insult and focused on what we needed to do instead. We would deal with our contract later. We rode in silence the rest of the way. I relaxed my tensed muscles as soon as we crossed the entrance to my private garage. We'd made it. Caterina was safe. As long as she remained here, she would be okay, just like I had promised.

For tonight, I had hoped for a different kind of dinner for us, more like a date and less like an arrangement. But our run-in with possibly the FBI ruined my plans. She didn't get to change into her dress. I fisted my hands. Why was it that when it came to Caterina, nothing ever went the way I wanted it? Everything she touched had the ability to spin out of my control.

"Where are we going?" She finally spoke when we walked into the elevator car.

"Earlier today, we didn't get to finish our conversation."

When the doors slid open, I ushered her down the carmine corridor. The old building smell soothed me and helped me find my center again. Next to me, Caterina fidgeted as we walked toward the boardroom. Good, she remembered this room. The last time she had been here, she offered herself to me. I swallowed and put the erotic images of her out of my mind.

"What do you want from me?" She headed for her chair at the table, as if the piece of furniture could save her from me.

I ambled around her and found my seat. Bracing my hands on the new manila folder, I leaned toward her and smiled. She was finally here. "Here's a revised copy of the contract."

"Wait. What?" She knitted her brows in disapproval or confusion. Who the hell knew? "We got chased out of my apartment by someone who possibly wanted to hurt me. And all you can think about is getting your stupid contract signed?"

"I wanted to give you more time. But that's not going to happen now. This part of our deal needs to be done."

"Why?"

"Because you're not leaving here tonight. Not for a long time."

"What?"

"You're staying. And I don't think I can stand sleeping in the room next to you until we hash out our terms."

"You're insane."

"The fact remains." I pushed the papers toward her. "I need you to sign."

She thumbed through the pages. Every time she stopped at a particular page, she would purse her lips and shake her head. I leaned back and crossed my ankle over my leg. After a long while, she closed the folder and glanced up at me. "You literally only changed two things."

"I conceded plenty on a lot of things."

She shook her head, and my heart raced. Was she going to say no?

"What happened today? Who was after me?"

"You don't need to concern yourself with that."

She rolled her eyes. "I can handle my own. I'm not your fragile pet." She motioned toward the contract. "Tell me. I won't sign until you do."

"I'm handling it."

She rose to her feet and headed toward the door. Jesus. I chased after her and slammed the door shut before she crossed the threshold.

"This is a familiar place." I cocked my head to look her in the eyes. "Maybe you'd like to make a different kind of deal."

My cock sure as hell wanted to. I braced my hands on either side of her head, pressing hard against the door to steel myself. She was such a distraction.

"What happened today? And don't lie."

"I don't lie." I stepped back. "Someone tried to kill Michael today. I got there just in time and shot the assailant in the knee. He got away."

"How's Dad?"

"He's fine. He's tougher than you think." I released a breath. Telling her about the incident made me feel lighter. "I called my personal bodyguard to send a cleaning crew to the hospital. Aaron saw the request, and thankfully, thought to stay closer to you to protect you until I got there. He did the right thing."

She stared at me with a blank expression. "I tossed his phone out the window and told him to go fetch." She tapped her head to the door, then her body jerked. "I need to see Dad."

"Not until we figure this out."

"You can't keep me here." She stood taller, glowering at me.

"I told you the truth." I extended my arm toward the table. "Or were you lying about signing after I told you what happened?"

"This is ridiculous." She practically stomped back to her chair. Her eyes watered as she picked up the pen I had left there for her and signed.

Hot adrenaline rushed through me. Suddenly, the air felt lighter, tasted sweeter. She was finally here. After two years, Caterina had agreed to come to me. She'd agreed to be mine. Yeah, the world was falling apart outside these walls. But at least now, we had each other.

"Why would you want your enemy living under your roof?" She surveyed the library on the other side of the room. "Tie me up. Tie me down. Nothing will change between us."

"We were never enemies, love."

"Yes, we are." She shot to her feet. "You're about to find out just how much. Because nowhere in that stupid contract does it say that I have to be nice to you."

I rubbed the stubble on my cheek. "Today was a long, fucked-up day. Let's end it right. My assistant will help you get ready."

CHAPTER 13
If You Want, We Could Make It Real

CATERINA

I had signed the contract. As of now, I was Rex's plaything for the next six months. He had agreed to reduce the time of our arrangement, but he didn't concede on letting me return to the office. Not that it mattered if he was getting ready to buy the company and sell it for parts. At least now I could talk to Dad and tell him he was free of Rex. The stress of his debt was literally killing him.

"I want to see Dad."

"Do you understand what's happening?"

"Sure I do. I'm not an idiot. Somehow, the Society is under attack. And even though Dad and I have nothing to do with it, we're being targeted just the same."

He prowled closer to me, and I crossed my arms in front of me. Tonight, his smell had an added hint of danger and sweat. And damn if that wasn't intoxicating and distracting. Holding my breath, I stepped away, but all he had to do was reach out to bring me back into his circle. How was I going to survive six months of him being this close?

"That's correct. Except for one thing." He brushed a strand of hair away from my cheek. "You have everything to do with the Society."

I glared at him, hoping he could see how much I despised him. "It's all because of you. This is all your doing."

"If you need to pretend Michael had nothing to do with your current predicament, fine. I'll let you be." His sexy stubble made a scratchy noise when he rubbed his fingers along his jaw. "Are you hungry?"

"No."

He rolled his eyes. "You will join me for dinner later."

"I don't think so. Meals were not in the contract."

A small win. If I could call it that. But something in his infuriating smirk made want to hurt him with pettiness. He grabbed his phone off the table and tapped on it. "How's this for items not in the contract?" He showed me the screen. When Nurse Sam appeared, I reached for the device, but he held it at arm's length. "Your time with me can be as hard or as pleasurable as you make it. Just remember that."

"Why do you hate Dad so much? I know you're doing this to hurt him." I jerked my chin toward the stupid contract.

"I don't hate him." His eyes softened. "Not anymore."

"Ms. Alfera. How are you?" Sam waved at me from the screen and saved me from yet another argument with Rex.

"How is he?" I stepped closer to him, or Rex really, since he was still holding the phone.

"Much better. Do you want to talk to him?"

I nodded with tears brimming my eyes. "Yes, please."

"Bells, are you okay?" Dad touched a hand to the device. I

116

imagined him brushing my cheek to soothe me. He didn't look like someone who had almost been murdered. "Sam says the surgery went well. But I still have a long road ahead before I'm back to normal."

"That's great, Dad." I beamed at him, wiping my face.

"Bells, don't worry about me. I'm well taken care of here."

I opened my mouth to remind him that someone had managed to sneak into his room earlier today, but instead, I glanced up at Rex, silently asking the question—was he safe? How did we know we wouldn't have a repeat of today's incident?

"He's at a private clinic nearby. Sam and twelve of my most trusted men are with him."

"Thank you," I mumbled. Having Dad wedged between us added a layer of awkwardness to our already unorthodox arrangement. For Dad's sake, I felt like I needed to be nice to Rex.

"Please remind Rex of the promise he made to me. I'll see you soon. Okay?"

"What promise?" I asked, but Dad was already gone. I shifted my gaze to Rex's. "What promise? And don't tell me you don't want me to worry my little head with details. If it has to do with Dad, I need to know."

"Fine." He motioned for me to sit down then lowered himself on his high-back chair.

He fit so well perched on his throne in this old-world room. When he hesitated again, I braced myself for the worse. "I can handle it. Whatever it is."

"Michael is sure that whoever is after him will come for his family too." He inhaled. "I think we can all agree he's right in that, given what happened at your place. He wants me to find your brothers."

I beamed at him. Enzo and Massimo had been gone for two years since Mom passed away. "Don't waste your time." I took a seat. "I tried calling them when Dad had the heart attack. I got nothing. They don't care."

"I'll make them care." He reached for my hand.

His soft caress unraveled something inside me. I supposed if anyone could bring my brothers back to New York, it would be the all-powerful Rex. "Why would you do that?"

"I made a promise." He smiled at our intertwined fingers. "I'll need one thing in return."

I pulled away from him, but he tightened his grip. He already had a signed contract that made me his plaything for half a year. What else could he want? Sex? He had said he didn't pay for sex, but technically finding my brothers was more of a favor. I squeezed my legs together, hating my body for the way it responded, the way it melted every time Rex was near. Did it not understand Rex was bad for our health?

He chuckled, jerking me back to reality before my imagination flashed more images of the last time Rex kissed me. "I know what you're thinking. But it isn't that." He tugged at the hem of my shirt and my nipples perked up. "I want your help."

"What?" I furrowed my brows. "What could I possibly do for you?"

"It seems that after today's attack, you and I have a common goal." He shot a glance toward the ceiling as if looking for the right words. "Even if Michael made a deal with the devil to leave the Society, you're still part of it. Your brothers too. Because whoever is after us, didn't get the memo that your family bailed."

"What do you want from me?"

"Join me. Publicly. Show the other families that the Alferas have agreed to a truce with me. I need us to work together. I can't be watching my back while fighting off the FBI."

"The FBI tried to kill Dad?" I placed a hand over my mouth. They were supposed to be the good guys. How could they try to assassinate an old man who had just had surgery?

"It's all speculation at this point. But we need to operate under that assumption until we prove otherwise. I need you." He squeezed my fingers.

For the first time since I met Rex, he was asking instead of demanding. The simple gesture warmed me to my core. But beyond that, he was right. Whether we considered ourselves part of this mafia family or not, my family was implicated in this new war with the FBI. If I wanted us to survive, I had to agree to Rex's request for a truce.

"Okay. I'll do whatever you want."

He sat back in his chair and puffed out a breath. "I have a few guests coming today. All you have to do is make an appearance with me."

"Are you serious? Do you ever sleep?" I checked the time on the grandfather clock behind me. "We're well into the evening."

"Did you think mobsters kept office hours?"

"I don't know what I thought." I rose to my feet. "Is this what I'm to expect? A run in with the FBI in the morning, then sex parties at night?"

He fisted his hands and stood. The look in his eyes said he was more determined than mad. "There's someone I want you to meet. I want her to see us together."

"I thought you said you didn't lie." I braced my hands on my hips just because I knew that rubbed him the wrong way. "You know for someone who doesn't lie, you sure spend a lot of time manipulating the truth. Which you ought to know is the same as lying."

In two strides, he closed the space between us and wrapped his arm around my waist. My body more or less slammed against his hard chest. "Rex." I panted a breath and slightly pushed away at his shoulders.

"If you want, we could make it real." He ghosted my lips, then moved over to my cheek and went on. "Every time you say my name, my resolve goes out the window."

His hands lingered on my lower back for several beats as if he were trying to decide if he wanted to take me on the table like he had said before or not. Or maybe he was waiting for me to make the first move. Meanwhile, my throbbing clit had already come up with a bunch of bad ideas—like what would happen if I shifted half an inch and let him kiss me again? I inhaled, and he dropped his hands so fast I thought maybe someone had come in. But when I checked, we were still alone.

"You hanging from my arm should do the trick." He lowered his gaze down to my core for a split second before he added, "You'll need to change."

"I didn't bring any clothes."

He smiled. A genuine gesture that made the temperature in the room go up several degrees. "You'll find what you need in your room. I'll walk you." He ambled toward the door and swung it open.

Outside in the vestibule, he let out a breath while he surveyed the end of the hallway as if considering something. I had been in this part of the building a few times now. I knew the elevator bay up to his penthouse was straight ahead.

"I think it'll be a good idea for you to learn where the secret passages are. There's a door through there." He pointed at the far corner of the antechamber. "The stairs will take you up to the penthouse."

"Okay."

"Let's go through there now."

He pushed on the wooden panel, and a skinny door swung open. The stairwell went up and down. I knew he was two floors up, so I headed that way. The cement steps and steel rails were a stark contrast to the room we had left behind with its silk wallpaper, huge fireplace, and antique looking furniture. This section of the building was meant as an escape route, not to impress guests.

When we reached Rex's floor, he punched in a number in the security keypad and then pulled on the door. On the other side of the wall, we were in a small lobby with a shimmering chandelier hanging overhead. Here, we were back in modern-day times with a decor that was fresh and sleek with beige walls and shiny marble floors. I followed him to the massive double doors on the left.

This had to be the front entrance to his penthouse. "Do I get a key?"

"No." He deadpanned and pushed the door open.

The elevator we had used yesterday was to my right, facing the grand staircase that led to the upper bedrooms. My heart rate spiked when I realized that the gray and beige color scheme of his living room, the marble fireplace, and the city view felt familiar to me.

"You'll be staying in the same room as before." He

motioned toward the steps. "It should be unlocked." He stayed close to me as we went up the steps and down the wide corridor adorned with tall mirrors and fresh floral arrangements. "I'm right next to you. I'll come and knock in half an hour."

I stood there and watched him go into his own suite. At least he wasn't expecting me to share a bed with him. That would've been creepy. And agonizing for me. Shaking my head to clear my dirty thoughts of Rex sleeping next to me, I strode inside the bedroom. Everything looked exactly as before with the bed on one side and a seating area on the other. The sofa and bedding decor were posh, done in creams and grays.

Making my way to the bathroom, I half-expected Rex's assistant to jump out. She didn't, and I was grateful for that. I didn't need any witnesses tonight watching me officially become Rex's mafia doll. He hadn't even flinched or shown a modicum of contrition when he said he just wanted me to hang from his arm.

Like last night, I showered quickly and slipped into a fluffy bathrobe. There was no escaping for me tonight. It occurred to me that, that was probably why Mary Anne hadn't been here. Rex knew I wasn't going to run away from him this time.

I put my hair up in a loose side French braid and made use of the toiletries and makeup in the vanity, before I headed to the adjacent room to pick something to wear. Since my power suit from work wasn't good enough for Rex and his guests, I had to assume he wanted me in a cocktail dress. I ambled into the walk-in closet and froze, glaring at the single garment hanging there, a corseted dress in a rust color.

The sheer top fit tight around the waist while the skirt was feathery and flowy with a slit that went up to my crotch. Luckily, the outfit came with matching underwear. It was a sexy number. I had to give him that. I puffed out a breath and donned the dress, the matching Jimmy Choos and the diamond bracelet. Basically, every item found in the closet.

Twenty-nine minutes and fifty seconds later, Rex knocked on my door. Pacing the room, I fidgeted with my attire, knowing I was being petty for making him wait. It was his own party. He could be late if he wanted. He rapped again. Harder this time.

"Caterina." He called for me, and I stood my ground. "Jesus fuck, Caterina. If she left, I swear..."

A string of profanities in Italian echoed out in the hallway. I didn't speak the language, but I knew a few of those words. He slammed his hand on the door one more time right before he barged in with a wild look in his eyes. When he saw me standing in the middle of the room, he stopped in his tracks and raked a hand over his perfectly styled hair. The man should not be allowed to wear a tuxedo. It wasn't fair how it made his blue eyes look even bluer, deeper, and more intense.

"I'm ready." I pointed at the dress suddenly regretting my pettiness. "This was all I found in there."

Slowly, he prowled toward me and cradled my neck. "Beautiful."

My toes curled when his hot breath fluttered on my face and deep down into my cleavage. Rex's world was unfamiliar, layered with danger and mystery. Everything about this place made me want to run out and never look back. But his touch made me feel like I could do this. I felt safe here with him.

I caught a glimpse of my reflection in the full-size mirror by the bathroom door. How the hell was I going to survive six months of this? More importantly, how was I supposed to help

Dad and my brothers, while still keeping my sanity and my sense of self? Because one thing was for certain, when Rex asked for my utter surrender, he not only meant my body and mind. By the way his gaze roamed every inch of me now, I knew he meant to unequivocally claim my heart and soul too.

CHAPTER 14
Bunny, Bun, Hun

CATERINA

Rex ushered me to his private elevator. As we made our way down to the Crucible level, I braced myself for another round of Rex's sex club. But when the car door slid open, we were on a different floor. The warehouse style room had floor-to-ceiling windows that offered a fantastic view of the city. Not that any of the patrons noticed it as they kept their gazes glued to their cards. This had to be the place where Dad lost millions of dollars gambling.

The music played in the background, but not too loud that it was impossible to carry a conversation. Not that Rex had anything to say to me after he found me in my suite. The whole way here, he kept his hand firmly on my waist, as if he were afraid I might take off if he didn't. He expertly maneuvered me through the gaming tables and sitting areas until we reached the bar, which covered the entire length of the room.

"Is she here yet?" His long fingers tapped on the counter as he waited impatiently for the bartender to turn around and answer. He had leaned away from me, but his arm stayed tightly wrapped around me.

"Yes, sir. She was here a minute ago."

"Good." Rex returned his attention to me. His gaze dropped to my cleavage then up to my lips before he pressed his mouth to my temple. "You really do look stunning in that dress."

"Rex." I wedged my arm between us. His proximity and soft tone were a huge turn on. Why?

He groaned and pulled me even closer to him. "Don't say my name unless you mean it."

"What am I supposed to call you?" I fired back. "My liege?"

"That has a nice ring to it coming from your lips." He slid his thumb across my cheek.

A spark of heat unraveled below my navel. Was this him pretending we were together? Or was this just another game of his to torture me? My body didn't care either way. Real or not, I melted into him and got lost in the gleam of his eyes. The man was infuriatingly hot.

His hand slid down to cover the column of my neck. "I'm very much looking forward to our first session later tonight."

What? The room swayed a few times as the words fully registered in my mind. He had meant a bondage session. He meant to do all those things from the pictures to me in a few hours. Suddenly, I couldn't breathe as I imagined myself in those photos. Tightly roped with my arms behind my back, suspended several feet off the ground. My body twirling round and round in a dark room.

"Shh." Rex cradled my face as he ghosted my slack mouth. "Don't be afraid."

"So, the rumors are true." A woman with a deep smoker's voice appeared in my peripheral vision. "Caterina Alfera has come home."

The middle-aged woman adjusted the mink shawl over her proud shoulders as she studied me with curiosity. She wore a black sequined floor-length gown that made her look ten feet tall. Her gray hair was twisted into a chignon. It sat on her head like some sort of crown. Everything about her, her presence, her energy, and even the way she held her hands screamed power and old money.

A wicked smile pulled on Rex's lips before he turned to face her. "Signoria Vittoria. I'm glad you could make it." He glanced down at me. "I don't believe you have been properly introduced."

"Caterina. This is Vittoria Salvatore." He offered her a curt nod. "She represents the Salvatore family."

The woman was a Don.

"È un piacere conoscerti, dolce bambina." She took my hand in hers as her gaze bore into mine, as if trying to look into my soul or maybe drink from it.

Vittoria scared the crap out of me.

"Nice to me you too," I replied in English.

Even though I understood a few words, I didn't really speak Italian. Dad was fluent, but he never spoke the language around the house. I supposed that was his way of letting go of this mafia world, to prove to Mom he was really out. Though, now that I had met Rex and Vittoria, I could see that whatever Dad and Mom thought they had outside of the Society was just an illusion.

"I never thought I'd see the day. I'm happy to be proven wrong." She squeezed Rex's arm and smiled. A gesture that had a tinge of warmth to it. Of course, the older lady had a soft spot for Rex. "My niece will be devastated."

"Which reminds me. Last night you left in such a hurry, we didn't get to finish our conversation." Rex motioned toward the grand staircase behind her.

The upper-level loft offered a view of the entire floor. But more importantly, it was private—for very important people only. I tried to remain cool, but this was too much for me. Rex wanted my help. But if he wanted me to talk to Vittoria or convince her of anything, he had the wrong girl.

"I believe you're right." She smirked at me.

Rex placed his hand on the bar, and that was all the bartender needed to rush toward us. "Caterina will have a glass of rosé. Send a bottle of Macallan upstairs."

When he faced me, he removed his arm from around my waist. Losing his support made me feel lost and cold.

"I had hoped to leave you in good company." He scanned the room and pursed his lips. "I'm sorry." He brushed my cheek with his lips. "Stay here. I'll find you when I'm finished with Vittoria."

Finished? Something twisted in my gut. I knitted my brows at him in confusion. No, I wasn't jealous, of course not. But if he was supposed to be here with me, I was curious to know what kind of business he had to finish with Vittoria and a bottle of expensive whiskey in the VIP loft.

"Take all the time you need." I took the wine the bartender set in front of me and took a long swig.

"I like this look on you." He flashed me a knowing smile as he brought my fingers to his wet lips.

"Get over yourself."

Whatever he thought was going on, he was dead wrong. I

watched him as he escorted Vittoria to the empty and dim-lit loft. I spun to face the bar and drank some more, glaring at my reflection in the mirror wall. My eyes watered, and I swallowed. This place wasn't for me. This wasn't my world. I belonged out there where the real people lived. This twisted and dark fairytale world was more than I could handle. No wonder Mom couldn't wait to get out—why she did everything she could to make sure we would never need a favor from the mob.

"There you are."

I glanced up and spotted a face in the mirror just over my shoulder. She seemed familiar, but I couldn't quite place her face. "Hi, I'm Violet." She plopped herself on the barstool next to mine. "You're Caterina?"

Shit. Rex's former bottom. The five-star rater. The one who wrote me a two-page letter on how great Rex was at being a top.

"Rex asked me to talk to you." She beamed at me.

I shifted my body to get a better look of the VIP section. Rex appeared at the top of the stairs with his phone pressed to his ear. Right away, Violet's phone rang in her purse. Her cheeks flushed as she pulled out her mobile and faced Rex.

"Hey." She nodded, turned to me, and handed me the phone. "He wants you."

Shit. I had let Rex bring me here and didn't even think to ask him for my phone. Come to think of it, I hadn't even brought my bag with me. "I left my stuff at my apartment." I spoke into the speaker.

"I know. Aaron will get it for you." He took a long pause while he watched me from the loft. "I'd like for you to spend some time with Violet. Would you do it?"

"Why?" My gaze shifted from Rex's tall form to Violet's eager face.

"I don't want you to be scared about tonight." He said matter-of-factly.

"Oh. Um. Fine."

What choice did I really have?

As soon as I agreed to his request, he hung up. I tilted my head in his direction, but he was already gone. I let out a breath. Between sleeping at the hospital, working, and spending hours going through Rex's contract, I was beyond exhausted. Didn't he feel tired too? He had spent his afternoon chasing bad guys. How was he still in the mood for kink?

"Hey, bunny." Violet bumped her shoulder against mine. When I rose both eyebrows in surprise, she clicked her teeth. "Bunny, bun...hun. I'll just call you hun."

"Caterina works."

"I was just trying to break the ice. I can see you're nervous. Don't be. Rex is the best rigger I've ever had." She beamed at me. "I was honored when he asked me to help you out."

"What exactly are you helping me with?" I sipped my wine.

"Like I said in my letter." She jumped off her seat and went to stand behind me. "Face the mirror." She pointed toward the wall lined with liquor bottles then started massaging my neck. "Relax."

I made to push her hand away. It was eerie to have a complete stranger touch me with such familiarity in a public place. But then she hit a particularly tight knot along my shoulder, and I loosened up, practically melted into her.

"Rex was right. You carry the weight of the world on your shoulders." She bent her head to meet my gaze in the mirror. "I bet your hips are super tight too." She swapped hands so her left fingers rubbed the bundle of nerves near my spine while her other hand kneaded my hip.

Again, if we weren't in a gambling house, all of this would've been heaven. She worked her magic until I remembered where we were. A cold shiver ran through me at the thought that other people might know who Violet was. If they did, they would guess why I was here and what Rex planned to do to me later on.

"Whoa." She pulled away. "You're making yourself all stiff for no reason. We'll keep working on that in the morning." She patted my shoulder blades then hopped on the barstool. "What are you worried about? Talk to me."

"Fine. You want to know?" I shot a glance behind me. "It's humiliating. He's doing this to punish me. He hates me, my family, my father more than anyone."

"Oh, hun." She rubbed my cold arm a few times. "He's doing this for you. Not to you. Humiliation has nothing to do with it." Her kind smile was full of pity. As if I were some lost girl who needed someone like Rex to save me. "Give him a chance."

"Do you know what he is?" I cleared my throat. "I mean apart from his kink. Do you know what he does for a living?"

She needed to understand Rex wasn't some nice guy who wanted to help me. He had literally paid a million dollars to get me to take off my clothes and let him tie me up into a pretzel. Or whatever those positions were on the pictures he showed me.

"What does one thing have to do with the other?" She furrowed her brows at me. "I see he has his work cut out for him. Here's my advice. Go to him with an open mind. We'll talk again tomorrow."

"Tomorrow? Why?"

"I'm going to be your body awareness instructor. Did he not tell you that?"

"No. He didn't. Or maybe he did. I don't know." I rubbed my temples to ease the avalanche of scary images flooding my mind. Six months was a fucking long time.

The bartender brought me another glass of wine. When I reached for it, Rex's hand appeared out of nowhere and slid it away from me. "I think one glass is enough for tonight."

"Excuse me." I pursed my lips and shot him a nasty glance. It was one thing to tell me what to wear, but to tell me how much I could or couldn't drink, that was my absolute limit.

"I need you sober for later." He didn't even try to lower his voice, so Violet wouldn't hear him.

"Why?"

"I can't have your consent while you're impaired. Did you ladies have a good talk?" He directed his question at Violet.

"We did." Violet took my hand in hers. "You're right. She's so tense. Her whole right side is one big knot."

"Yes, she is." He met my gaze.

"What does that even mean?" Acid burned at the pit of my stomach at the idea that Rex had talked to Violet about me and what he thought of my body.

"I'll explain everything in the morning." She patted my wrist and slid off her barstool. "I'll see you bright and early tomorrow."

"Yeah, okay." I watched her as she planted a kiss on Rex's cheek, and then, disappeared into the crowd.

"Are you ready to go?" Rex wrapped his arm around my waist and pulled me off the seat.

Heat rushed to my cheeks at the huge implication of his question. Was I ready for a session with him? Hell no. But also, I didn't want to stay here and risk running into another one of his friends. How many ex-bottoms did he plan to bring in to teach me?

"I thought you said later." I wedged my hand between us, putting emphasis on the later part of my comment. I hoped my scowl reminded him of how much I despised him, how much I didn't want to be here with him, how much he was hurting me. "I think I want to stay. I mean, I would love to meet more of your girlfriends."

"I know what I said. But I can't wait any longer." He bent down and brushed his nose to mine. "And for the record, Vittoria and Violet are not my girlfriends, or ex-girlfriends for that matter. At least not in the sense your tone implied." He chuckled. "I'm sure Vittoria would get a kick out of that."

"I can't do this." I pressed my hand to my forehead, while my heart threatened to break my ribs. "Don't make me do this."

Rex wrapped his arms around me until he was supporting most of my weight. "Walk," he ordered as he ushered me through the crowd. Prada pumps and expensive Italian leather shoes whooshed in and out of my line of sight until they became a blur. I squeezed my eyes shut and focused on breathing or rather on the fact that I couldn't breathe. Before I knew it, we were back upstairs in Rex's penthouse. And I was all alone.

I crossed the threshold with his body close behind me. I turned around and held his gaze. His features relaxed as he reached for my cheek. Was that a smile? He had thought he had won, which technically he had, but did he have to be so smug about it?

"Rex." I snaked my hand inside his tuxedo jacket.

My fingers touched the cold handle of his gun, and I lost it. In a moment of pure insanity and a lame attempt to remain in control, I grabbed his weapon and aimed at his heart.

CHAPTER 15
Face the Mirror

REX

"What do you plan to do with that?" I put my hands up in surrender.

My heart pumped hard with exasperation and desire. That was how Caterina made me feel all the goddamn time. Why did she refuse to listen to me? Trust me? Why couldn't I stop wanting her? There were literally a dozen women downstairs waiting for me to invite them up to my penthouse. My life would be so much easier if I could stop thinking about Caterina Alfera.

"Let me go. Now."

"You know I can't do that." I stalked toward her. "One, there's a target on your back. You wouldn't last a day out there. And two, your father hasn't paid his debt."

"I don't care." She gritted her teeth, treating me to one of her "I hate you" glares.

"You're not the first one to pull a gun on me. Or shoot me for that matter." I stepped into her personal space, and she pressed the barrel of my gun to my chest. "You don't want to kill me. I can see it in your beautiful green eyes."

"Rex." She backed away, still holding my firearm but with less conviction than before.

"This is about the rope session. You're afraid you might enjoy it."

She shook her head.

"You're afraid you might like me. You're afraid that maybe you don't hate me as much as you say." I ghosted her lips. A beat later, she melted into me, and I pressed on. "You're ready."

"Rex."

"Stop saying my name." Really, every time she uttered that one word, I felt my resolve fading and giving in to her.

She braced her hand on my pecs, pushing me away but also digging her nails in. I bet she was wet and ready for me. When I didn't bend down to kiss, her cheeks flushed a bright red. The disappointment in her eyes cut me. It disarmed me. She disarmed me.

Fuck it.

I crushed my mouth to hers. She opened slightly with a quiet moan and grazed her teeth over my bottom lip. The taste of wine on her tongue sent me on a downward spiral. My thigh rubbed against her core as I walked her backward, slowly, until the sofa cut us off. Caging her with my body, I gripped her wrist and peeled the gun from her fingers.

"I need you," I whispered and deepened the kiss. "You need me too. Don't lie."

In my mind, I had already turned her around and undone her dress. I had kissed her mouth and neck until she begged me to fuck her hard. If she asked me, if she said those two little words...fuck me...I knew I wouldn't be able to say no. Jesus Christ, I had to get her upstairs before all my plans went to hell.

I pulled away, panting to catch my breath. "There's a change of clothes waiting for you in your suite. You have ten minutes. Leave your hair the way it is." It physically hurt to step back and drop my hands to my sides. "Go."

"You're such a jerk." She snatched the skirt of her gown from between my legs and darted to the grand staircase.

I stood there filled with anticipation as she disappeared in the hallway beyond the landing. Savoring the moment, I followed her. This had always been our dance. Ever since we reconnected after I came back from college. The push and pull of her feelings toward me were maddening.

She wanted me. That much I knew. But her instincts told her any kind of relationship with me would be bad for her. She wasn't wrong. All that was about to change. Because now, I had a way to communicate with her. Really speak to her outside of what our lives were supposed to be—outside of our obligation to the Society.

I shortened my gait in front of her door. The flutters in my chest threatened to spin out of control. So much was riding on this first session. If I could get Caterina to understand this new language, we might stand a chance. Smiling, I rushed to my own bedroom next door to hers and quickly removed my tuxedo, shoes, and socks. I donned a pair of grey sweats and nothing else, then paced the length of the room while I waited another minute to go see her.

At exactly ten minutes, I rapped on her door. This time, she didn't make me wait like before. She had finally understood that all the petty tantrums in the world could not change my plans for her. Not tonight. *Not ever.*

She stood at the threshold, proud and incredibly sexy in those tight, black yoga shorts and cami. Her cheeks blushed a pretty red. And in that moment, I decided we would start with a champagne, rose color rope to match her sun-kissed skin.

"We're not going far." I motioned toward the door across the hallway.

"I didn't think we would." She ogled me, blinking fast several times. "I'd never seen you this casual."

"I'm dressed for the occasion." I beamed at her.

"Can we just get this over with?" She side-stepped me to make sure she didn't touch me.

"What happened? First you want to leave. Now you're in a hurry to get tied up?"

She stopped in front of the rope room. "You enjoy the chase. I decided not to give you that anymore. Do your worst."

I dug a gold key out of my pocket and slipped it into the lock. When the door swung open, she knitted her brows at me.

"I think you made up a whole story in your head about what rope sessions are. Are you disappointed?" I ushered her into the mostly bare suite.

"No bed?"

"We won't need it." I sauntered to the side wall where I kept bundles of coiled rope and grabbed the pale rose one. I took my time to give her time to explore the room.

"Is that Central Park?" She walked to the tall windows, rubbing her arm.

"Yes." I inhaled the sweetgrass scented air and stood on the yoga mat positioned in front of the floor-length framed mirror. "Get on your knees."

She spun around, pursing her lips. "Yes sir." She rolled her eyes. "Is that what I'm supposed to call you?"

"Rex is fine."

"I thought you didn't like me using your name." Her bare feet slapped on the warm hardwood floors as she ambled toward me.

"I'm in control in this room. And starting now, you will only speak when I ask you a direct question. On your knees." I gestured toward the mat.

Her gaze shifted to the floor. After a few erratic breaths, she kneeled facing me. Under the soft flickers of the chandelier, her skin shimmered like the city lights beyond the windows. She was such a distraction. I had to call on my extensive training to control my breathing and focus on our session.

I fisted her hair at the nape of her neck and pulled gently to make her meet my eyes. Yeah, the fire and the hate were still there. "Face the mirror."

When she shifted her body, I dropped to my knees and cuddled her from behind, watching her reaction across the way. Her chest rose and fell as she waited for my next move. I sat on my ankles and pulled on her waist to gently invite her to do the same. She obeyed with a big exhale, as if she had been afraid we would explode if our bare skin touched.

Her smooth skin on my chest was everything I thought it would be. Normally, at this point of the session, I would ask my partner to close her eyes and focus on her breathing. But I couldn't do that just yet with Caterina. I craved for her to look at me in this setting. I needed to see that she wasn't scared of me, and what I was. She knew I was a mobster, a beast in a world of criminals. And in a way, she understood I had to be this way.

But rope practice was a completely different matter because she didn't know how I had ended up here—why kinbaku had become integral to my survival.

I dug into my pocket and removed my phone, a pair of rope shears, and an hourglass timer. When I glanced up at her reflection, her eyes were big, and she had stopped breathing.

"These items—" I slid everything to the top of the mat, away from us but still within reach, "—are for your safety. Our hour starts now. You move when I move you and you breathe when I say, how I say. Let me do the thinking for you. Whatever is waiting for you outside this room, it'll be there when you wake up. Do you understand? Yes or no."

She met my gaze in the mirror, then glanced down at the jute snaking down her leg. I pressed on her hip, and her lips parted, but no words came out. We sat at a standoff for a few beats before she finally conceded.

"Yes." She let her side rest on my forearm, melting into me, all smooth skin and soft heartbeats.

That was it.

I had her.

She was mine.

Placing my palm across her clavicle, I flipped the hourglass with my free hand. "Take a deep breath and hold it. Keep it there."

When she released a bit of air, I held her tighter and let the tail ends of the rope fall on her bare thighs again, a little forceful this time.

"Exhale and close your eyes."

My hand trembled in anticipation as I held her wrists and quickly did a single-column bind on them. While I used my whole body to keep her contained, I brought her hands together against her sternum. "Match your inhales to mine."

Her head lulled to the side and rested on the curve of my neck and shoulder. I filled my lungs with air, and she did the same. That was my cue to add more intensity to our session. Using my whole body to box her in, I wound the rope around her body twice, tight and fast. I knotted the jute at the center of her back and used the remaining rope to add her foot to the bind. All the while, I varied the rhythm like a dance—quick, quick, slow, quick, quick, slow—to keep her guessing, to keep her mind on me and no one else—not Michael, her brothers, or her dead mother—just me.

In this moment, I was the only one who existed in her world. A surge of adrenaline washed over me. Having this much control over Caterina Alfera made me feel like I could take over the world. All my worries, all the people dying around me, all the chaos was muted and minimized by this power spiraling through me.

All my fantasies of Caterina in this very pose paled in comparison to the real thing. Her body heat and the scent of her arousal were something I hadn't considered. My heartbeat spiked as desire unfurled below my navel. I had to use all my training to reel it in and calm the fuck down.

I gripped her French braid, nudging my arm along her spine to push her away from me. The cold air that brushed between us helped me regain control. She was a vision in this pose, her neck long and silky, her chest heaving, and brows furrowed. She leaned back, looking for my body heat, but I held her in place, wedging my elbow into the middle of her spine. I wanted her to experience this sensation on her own.

The bind of the jute on her skin combined with the stretch

was a delicious kind of pain that I knew she would enjoy. Even if she refused to admit it, Caterina and I were so much alike. She needed this as much as I did. Her whole body screamed exactly that.

I flipped the rope over her shoulder and ran it just below her jaw. Pressing my lips to her skin, I exhaled a hot breath on her cheek. When she breathed exactly like me, I released the cord off her throat. The fact that she didn't flinch with the slight choke of the bind meant she trusted me completely.

Jesus fuck, now that I had her surrender, I wanted more of her. I wanted to bury my cock deep inside her and show her all the things we could have together. I wanted to make her come while she said my name over and over. I moved her head to the side and ghosted her lips. She squeezed her legs together, mouthing, "Rex."

"I'm right here." I wrapped one arm around her, unraveled the rope, and let it cascade around her. "I've always been here...Wake up," I whispered in her ear.

Her eyes flew open. When she met my gaze in the mirror, she blinked a few times, then shot a glance toward the hourglass. Our time was up, and it had been everything I thought it would be with her. Now I had no doubt she was my queen. Even though we were thrown together by circumstance, we were always meant for each other. The biggest question now was—did she agree?

She shifted her body away from me and turned to face me. Even though she was free to go, she remained on her knees with her hands planted firmly on the floor as if she were afraid that if she let go, she would fall. Her eyes watered and slowly filled up with the usual anger and hate. If she had shot me downstairs with my own gun, it would've been less painful.

"You can go." I stood with my arms crossed tight over my chest.

She opened her mouth to speak but no words came out. Instead, she glowered at me with a slight tremble to her lip. I could see she had a million things going through her mind. No doubt half of those were insults she wanted to hurl my way.

"Breathe, Caterina." I reached for her, but she recoiled away from me.

"I hate you." She scrambled to her feet and ran out of the room.

I raked a hand through my hair and stared at the door. A part of me wanted to chase after her, but what good would it do? She had seen the real me and now there was no going back. Maybe I was wrong, and Caterina didn't have the ability to put her hate aside. All this time, I thought I could change her mind. I thought I could make her face her feelings and see we could make something whole out of our broken pieces.

How could I have been so wrong about her?

CHAPTER 16

His Heart Doesn't Work That Way

CATERINA

So that was his fucking plan? Make me want him only to show me how much he didn't want me back? I slammed the door shut behind me, relieved that he wasn't following me, that he was done torturing me for the night. I stomped to the middle of the room, facing the city lights.

Wait. What? I hugged my waist. When had I decided I wanted sex with Rex? Anger bubbled in the pit of my stomach. From the moment he said he wanted my surrender, when he kissed me, when he held my hand, he had planted that seed. But he never had any intention to go through with it and put out this fire burning in my core.

I sat on the bed, not bothering with the lights. A small shiver went through me, and slowly the hour I had spent with Rex came rushing back. The sultry music and his touch were tattooed on my skin now. It'd been hypnotic the way he moved me and made me feel complete, lighter, and without a care in the world. I let myself fall on the mattress. As disappointed and hurt as I felt when he dismissed me like I was nothing, I didn't want the feeling to go away. I wanted his body close to mine. I wanted *him*.

There had been a point in the session when I thought he was going to fuck me right on that mat in that empty, dim-lit room. My clit throbbed so painfully. If I had not been tightly bound, I would have thrown myself at him and begged him to take me already. What was wrong with me? He was the reason Dad was in the hospital—why my family was ruined.

I rolled into a fetal position and slipped my hand inside my pants. Burying my face on the pillow, I moaned at the sweet relief. Tears streamed down my cheeks as I conceded to the fantasy brewing in my head—his wide chest and slim hips became a bright image in my mind. He was all smooth skin and hard muscle. Just like I had done in the rope room, I surrendered my body to Rex, letting the memories of him and everything he did to me flood my senses all over again. His hot breath brushed my neck and rushed to where my fingers moved in a circular motion around my folds.

"Rex." I called for him in defiance. He didn't like me saying his name. So, I said it over and over.

I imagined his intense gaze on my sex while he rubbed me near my aching bud, but not quite giving me what I wanted. I thought about how he would be cruel in bed like that. How he would make me want him until I felt like I was going to explode. How he would touch every inch of me like he did before and kiss me until he left me breathless. And then, just when I couldn't take any more of that sweet torture, I knew he would palm my sex and bring me to orgasm. I did exactly that. With rough strokes, I pleasured myself until I came.

The release was over quickly, like striking a match that gets put out almost immediately by a gust of wind. Argh. I screamed into my pillow in exasperation. How could Rex toy with me like this? And how was it that in spite of how cruel and dismissive he could be, I still wanted him. My tears left wet spots on the pillow. I wanted to flip it over, but I was too exhausted to move. Instead, I squeezed my eyes shut and yelped into it. *Go to sleep. Go to sleep.* I tried to lull myself to go to sleep.

"My beautiful Caterina." Rex's voice echoed in the dark room as the mattress dipped under his weight.

My body jolted awake or back to full awareness. I tried to twist my body to get away from him, but he held me tight.

"What do you want?" I hardly recognized my hoarse voice.

"I heard screams. I wanted to make sure you weren't hurt." His arms felt so good around me.

He smelled of incense, the same woodsy smell from the rope room, and his own manly musk. Did he hear me come? Had I really screamed loud enough for him to catch me saying his name? Heat washed over me, followed by cold sweat. Had he seen me too?

"You're not alone, Caterina."

If that were the case, I wouldn't be here. I clung to his body, gripped his T-shirt and buried my face in his chest. And now my humiliation was complete. He had my surrender. And he knew exactly how much I wanted him. My eyes fluttered closed, while he caressed my jaw and neck.

———

"Wake up, hun." Violet's voice startled me awake.

What? I glanced down at the pillow where I was fisting the

sheets. Did Rex come to my room last night? Or did I dream the whole thing? I pressed a hand to my forehead. Jesus, the man was driving me crazy.

The bright sunlight seemed to be everywhere in the room, and it hurt my eyes. "What time is it?" I threw the covers over my head. Apparently at some point during the night, I had gotten under the bedding. Or did Rex tuck me in before he left?

"It's noon. Do you always sleep this late?" She set a tray of food on the side table. The coffee smelled amazing and made my belly rumble with hunger for the fluffy omelet on the plate.

"No, I actually never do." I reached for the mug and sipped. "Ah, thank you. What are you doing here?"

"Our body awareness session started two hours ago. You forgot, didn't you?" She plopped herself on the bed, beaming at me. "How was your first session?"

"Hmm...don't ask." My cheeks flushed at the way I had lusted over Rex last night. Heat rushed through me when I recalled that in my frenzy, I had masturbated to Rex, and that there was a huge possibility I had done it while he watched.

"That good." She laughed.

"Did you ever have sex with him?" I blurted out, then winced. "I'm sorry. That's none of my business."

"Once." She shrugged and slowly her smile faded. "It was a mistake. I got all confused and thought I was in love with him."

"What happened?" I grabbed the tray and started eating.

"Just that. One night he was at the Crucible. I went up to the VIP loft and begged him to take me. He did. But then told me we were done. He said he couldn't love me. Remember what I said in my letter? Enjoy your time with him, but under-

147

stand love isn't on the menu. His heart doesn't work that way. He was honest about that since the beginning."

"Why are you here then? Doesn't it bother you to be around him?" My anger returned. How could Rex toy with her emotions that way?

"That was over two years ago. I'm over it. I was in a really dark place when he met me. I owe him my life. My time with Rex healed me. Shibari was a huge part of that. He's just a beautiful memory. Not to mention, I'm with someone new. He loves me and I love him. So no, it doesn't bother me to see him. I'm here because I love the idea of introducing a new bunny to the community. I told you. I was honored that he asked me to help you."

"Shibari?"

"Oh, it's just another term for erotic rope bondage." She picked up a strawberry off the tray and fed it to me. "Finish up and we'll get started."

I finished my breakfast and darted to the bathroom to shower and brush my teeth. As much as I didn't want to do the training session for Rex, Violet's energy was infectious. I was curious to learn what she had to teach me. In the walk-in closet, I found a change of clothes—a buttery soft bodysuit that was basically tight short, shorts and a halter-top.

"Who brings in these outfits?" I met Violet out on the terrace.

I had been in the suite several times now and hadn't noticed the outdoor space before. Violet regarded the sunny view while she sat on an outdoor chaise with white sand cushions. She smiled at me when I joined her. "Mary Anne. She's very sneaky that one." She winked.

"I bet." So Violet knew Rex's assistant whose sole job

appeared to be to take care of his bottoms. "Was this your bedroom?"

"What do you mean, hun?"

"Before when um..." I trailed off.

It felt wrong to say, "when you were his." I didn't like the lump that churned in my stomach when I pictured the two of them together. And then I pictured piles and piles of manila folders and all the women he had invited to his rope room, all the women he had cuddled and tied up the way he had done with me. My body temperature went up a few degrees while I imagined doing another session and going through all those sensations all over again. I shook my head to clear my thoughts and focus on Violet.

"Oh no, hun. I went home every day." She cocked her head to meet my eyes. "Rex is very protective of his privacy."

"He helped me find a place not too far from here. He also got me a job. A good job."

Rex had helped her. As much as I liked to paint him as the villain, Violet's words didn't feel at odds with the man I had come to know. I could see him doing all those things for her. "What kind of trouble were you in before?"

"You know the usual, sex, drugs." She glanced down at her hands, shaking her head. "He dismantled one of those brothels. You know what I mean?"

I nodded.

"I had been working there for a year when he found me. I watched him kill a man that day...my pimp, I guess is the word." Her head snapped up at me. "Rex was kind to me, though. Like I said, he saved me."

"I'm so sorry." I wrapped my arm around her. "I'm glad he found you."

"Me too. I've been sober for three years now." She beamed at me. "Are you ready to get started?"

"Sure. Where do you want me?"

"Right here." She patted the seat. "I'm going to map your shoulders. It'll help you figure out how to breathe and where to position your arms during the binds."

I let out a breath, rubbing my temple. "I still can't get used to that terminology. Normal people don't use those words on a daily basis. Certainly not right after breakfast."

"Just keep an open mind." She chuckled.

Getting used to the idea of being Rex's bottom wasn't the problem. The real issue was my body thinking that Rex was on the menu. Twice, Violet had warned me against this. Rex could've asked any of his past bottoms to help him out. I was sure he had chosen Violet because of her experience with him. I needed to listen to her and stop wanting him this way. I had to remember that the rope sessions were just a kink to him, a game with his new plaything.

I spent the rest of the day with Violet doing hip flexor stretches and talking like we were old girlfriends. She was beautiful and funny. Every time she would crack a joke that had me in stitches, I couldn't help but wonder why Rex couldn't fall in love with her.

A soft knock on the door sent a rush of adrenaline through my body. I hadn't seen Rex since last night. I wasn't sure how I was going to face him again. "Come in." I shifted my weight on the mattress with my heart drumming in my throat.

Mary Anne strolled in with the outfit du jour for me, and I sat back on the pillows like a deflated balloon.

"Mr. Valentino would like for you to join him for dinner

tonight." She lifted the dress to eye level before she arranged the items on the upholstered chair near the window.

The last time we saw each other, I had been nice to her but only so she would let down her guard. I hoped my little escape stunt that night didn't get her in trouble. "I'm sorry about before." I glanced over at Violet sitting on the bed next to me with her legs stretched out in front of her.

"You were scared." She smiled at me with kindness in her eyes and shrugged, as if Rex brought frightened girls to his penthouse all the time. "Dinner is in an hour."

"Dinner? Omigod. I didn't realize it was so late." Violet scrambled across the bed and jumped to her feet. "I have to go."

"Why don't you stay?" I met Violet halfway to the door as soon as Mary Anne disappeared into the bathroom. "I would love the company."

She laughed. "I wish I could stay, but I have to go. I'll see you tomorrow." She threw an arm around my neck. "Be kind to yourself." She waved a finger to my eyebrows. "Even now I can see you're overthinking everything. Rex is offering you a gift, an escape of sorts. Take it." She kissed my cheek and left.

Blowing out a breath, I collapsed on the bed. I wasn't ready to see Rex again or to be in his arms. I flipped onto my belly to take a look at the clothes Rex had sent. It was a backless sheath dress with spaghetti straps. It reminded me of the cocktail number I wore when I threw myself at Rex the first time. Anger and shame fluttered in my gut at the memory. That night I had convinced myself I was doing it to save Dad from jail. And yeah, that part was true. But I would be lying to myself if I didn't admit that I had also been turned on by the idea of having sex with Rex, the ruthless mafia king who hated Dad.

"I can help you get ready." Mary Anne stood by the foot of the bed.

"No, thank you." I let my bare feet drop to the plush area rug beneath the bed. "I won't be needing help. Please let Mr. Valentino know I will not be joining him for dinner. I'm not hungry."

Mary Anne's eyes went wide in surprise. "Are you sure you want me to say that?"

"I am."

"I'll let him know." She gave me a quick nod and walked out.

The suite felt too quiet and too empty when the door shut behind her. I curled up on the bed and thought of Dad all alone in a hospital bed. Had Massimo and Enzo responded to my messages? Where the hell were they? Dad needed them. I needed them. Hot tears stung my eyes.

"You need to eat." Rex's voice jerked me back to reality.

"I'm not hungry." I rolled off the bed so I could glower at him properly. "You let Violet go home." I cringed at the whiny tone in my voice.

"She didn't have a target on her back like you do. You're here for your own safety." He closed the space between us and effectively sucked all the oxygen out of my lungs. "You will join me for dinner."

"And if I don't?" I met his gaze.

"We'll have to find a way to work up your appetite." He ghosted his lips along my jaw. His hot breath seeped down into my sports bra and then my pants. And just like that, I was wet and ready for him. He snaked his arm around my waist and whispered in my ear. "You still owe me an hour for today."

A raw charge sparked at the apex of my sex, and I melted into him. "Rex." I gripped the front of his T-shirt, and then, I realized he was dressed in a pair of dark gray sweats and no shoes.

"I tried to stay away. I swear I did." He wedged his thigh in between mine and walked me backward. "You should've said yes to dinner instead."

Before my brain could figure out what he was doing, I was in the middle of the hallway waiting for him to unlock the door to the rope room.

CHAPTER 17
He's Not on The Menu

CATERINA

He's not on the menu.

I repeated it several times in my head until the ruckus in my chest settled down. Warmth seeped through my bare feet as I padded across the heated hardwood floors. Behind me, Rex shut the door and walked over to the rope wall. I rubbed my temples and tried not to overthink things. Yeah, the man had a rope wall. That was normal in his world because he was Rex Valentino and that meant he could do whatever he damn well pleased.

I ambled toward a chic armless chaise, upholstered in dark blue velvet. On the gold side table, a dish with two incense sticks fused the air with an earthy scent. Had this piece of furniture been here before? I ran my hand over the smooth fabric. It had to have been because it all felt familiar. Last night I had been too nervous and too angry to really absorb all the details, though the sweetgrass scent had stayed with me for hours—on my skin and in my hair.

I turned around, and my gaze zeroed in on the floor-length mirror. That part I hadn't missed. Heat flushed across my skin as memories of what I saw in there last night reeled through my mind. We were about to do it all over again.

When I faced Rex, he reached behind him and pulled on his T-shirt. The city lights illuminated every plane on his chest and abs. Jesus, the man had the body of an Adonis. And now I knew how hard his pecs were. I knew how well I fit in his arms.

"On your knees." His commanding tone sent rays of want through me.

I closed the space between us. Something about being in a semi-dark room emboldened me. "What do you get out of this? I get it's a control thing for you. But if you plan on doing this to me for the next six months, you have to know how this makes me feel. Or is that it? You get your kicks by getting women to want you just so you can reject them?"

"Go on." He gestured toward the thick mat, ignoring my question.

In this room, his intense blue eyes were more serene and bright. He was in control of his emotions and my body. I hated that he could make me squirm with desire, while he remained unaffected by all of it.

"I forgot. No talking." I dropped to my knees.

"That's right."

The sequence of his movements was the same as last night. He kneeled behind me, then removed his phone, the hourglass, and a pair of shears from the pocket of his sweat-pants and placed them on top of the mat. The soft hair on his chest bristled across my back. I softened my body, molding myself to him—my head and hips and legs, they gently nestled into his space. Whatever happened an hour from now or in six months, I didn't care. I craved to feel alive again.

In the next beat, a slow piano tune began to play, and suddenly I was aware of his hands on my shoulders softly kneading and applying pressure below my shoulder blades. "Take a deep breath and hold it." His lips brushed the soft spot behind my ear and then went on. "Your skin is so soft, like velvet."

A slight burn gripped my chest, but I didn't dare let go of my breath. Not until he told me to.

"What do I get out of this? I get you, Caterina. All of you." He wrapped his arms around me and then guided my legs to crisscross in front of me as if I were his doll.

I supposed at this point in the session, I was his doll, his rope bottom, just his.

"Empty out your lungs...slowly...sweetly."

We did a few more rounds of breathing until it felt natural that our inhales and exhales kept the same rhythm. The tempo of the song increased, and a woman quietly sang in Italian. It was too fast for me to understand, but she sounded lonely. Rex snapped the coiled rope and let it fall on my leg. The hard feel of the jute on my thigh effectively stopped my mind from wandering off.

"Let me do the thinking for you." He brought my hands behind my back until my wrists crossed right in the middle. "Close your eyes."

The feel of the polished rope on my skin, the sound of it hitting the mat combined with the vibrations of it against my torso as he pulled the line through was a sensation like no other. And that was all my body and mind needed to surrender to Rex's wicked game. I watched in the mirror as he carefully wrapped the jute around my chest, then leaned into me while he kept his gaze glued to mine. He commanded the attention of all my senses in a way that was so erotic to me and a huge turn on.

He continued working on the tie, using a single hand to knot a second rope to the one he had going. Violet had given me instruction on a few simple harnesses. Rex had decided to do a box tie or takate kote tonight. I knew what was coming.

By the time he was ready, my shorts were drenched with want and anticipation. He paused for a breath, then firmly cupped my breast to secure the rope where he wanted it. A raw charge sparked at my core in response. His large hands fit perfectly around each mound as he repeated the process twice more. When he finished, my heart thrashed in my ears.

"Rex."

The name had become synonymous with "Please, I want you." Tears stung my eyes with frustration. But that didn't stop me from letting my mind wander to the place where Violet had warned me not to go.

"I know." With rough tugs and pulls, he secured the rope behind me. The stretch felt good on my arms, but the part that enclosed my breasts was agony. I wanted more than the pressure. I wanted his hands on me again. Instead of giving me what I needed, he yanked until my whole torso rested on his thighs and my tits were practically on display for him.

My aching nipples begged for his touch. If the smirk that played on his lips was any indication, he knew exactly how he affected me. "The scent of your arousal has become a drug to me." He snaked more cord in front of me, right over my taut peaks and then between my legs. "Why is it that with you, things never turn out the way I planned them?"

"Maybe because you made me come here. You made me your prisoner just to hurt me and..." I meant to say Dad. But in truth, he had no clue what I was going through, or all the things Rex had made me do to settle his debt. This thing was only between Rex and me. It was about us and no one else.

"And are you in pain right now?" He gripped my bound wrists and did another loop over my throbbing pussy.

When I realized I was so close to coming, a wave of heat rushed through me. It was a mix of shame and unadulterated desire.

"Answer."

"No." I panted a breath. "Please." I wanted to buck my hips toward his hand, but the position I was in made it so only he could move me. He decided how much sensation to give me and how much to take away. "Rex."

"I'm right here. And I'm not going anywhere." He rose to his knees and brought me up with him to face the mirror. I gasped and shut my eyes. I didn't want to see what I had become in his hands. "I want to see your green eyes when you climax. It'll be a nice change of pace from the usual hate they spew my way every time I get near you."

I shook my head. Everything with Rex had a price. The price of my release right now was my humiliation. He wanted me to watch him while he made me come. My clit screamed at me to say yes. Just this one time. Who cared if Rex won this round? Wasn't that always the case with him anyway? He always got what he wanted. It was why I was here, forty-five floors over Manhattan, literally trapped in an ivory tower.

"Open your eyes," he whispered. His hot breath scurried down my arm and made my sex pulse a little harder.

The woman in the mirror wasn't me. I didn't recognize the

wild look in her gaze or the messy waves cascading over her shoulders. My rib cage expanded with a rugged breath and made the tie rub over my nipples. I did it again to soothe me, and then again. It was a small act of defiance to sit here and pleasure myself when Rex refused to.

"What do you want me to do?" I asked when he didn't move.

"Just look at me."

I did. At this point I was so turned on and hot for him, it only took three strokes before my core exploded into a bouquet of hot waves that ravished every part of me. And it was like nothing I had ever felt. He continued to work me until every last bit of my orgasm was spent. The whole time, his gaze stayed locked onto mine. My bright eyes in the mirror betrayed me, offering him a glance of gratitude. I collapsed backward on his chest while tiny convulsions gripped my pussy and shot up into my breasts. Just then, Rex pulled at the rope around my wrists and the entire harness unraveled over my shoulders. For a second, an odd panic washed over me as I recalled Violet's words when I asked her if she'd had sex with Rex.

"His Heart Doesn't Work That Way"

I scrambled to my knees and turned to face him. Being this far from him hurt. The room was suddenly too cold and too empty. Would he leave now? Or tell me he was done with me? My eyes watered at the realization that I wanted Rex with me, that if he left now my heart would break in two.

"You're so fucking perfect." He cradled my cheek and crushed his mouth to mine.

He kissed me hard and desperately while I ran my hands over his chest and into his soft hair. Without asking or easing into it, he thrust his tongue past my lips, tasting me and egging me to do the same. I took what he offered because I knew it wouldn't last. Per his rules, this arrangement was over.

His skin smelled of incense and mint. I wanted all of him, but in the back of my mind, I steeled myself for what I was sure would come next. The hourglass was empty, and our time was up. He pulled away first and flashed me a knowing smile that made me want to slap him and then kiss him again.

"What happens now?" I pulled the collapsed harness over my head. After he had sex with Violet, he sent her away right after. Or at least, I imagined that was how it had happened since she didn't exactly elaborate. She did say, they only had done it once. "Is your little experiment over? Violet told me what happened with her."

"I figured she might." He rose to his feet. I supposed he wanted to hover over me so he could throw me out properly.

"I went too far." I licked my lips. Certainly, Rex watching me come on his rope counted as sex. I stood, though my stance didn't have the strength I had hoped for. For one, I had been tied down for almost an hour. And two, my clit was overly sensitive, like it expected another round—or two. I ran a hand through my hair to clear my thoughts. "I broke your rule."

He chuckled, rubbing the stubble on his cheek. "My little virgin. If you thought that was sex, you have much to learn." He stalked closer to me. "When you and I have sex, you won't have a single doubt that we indeed had sex. Now that you're here, I'm not letting you go. When are you going to understand that?"

When? Why did it seem like he had said sex a hundred times?

"Stop saying that word." I made to leave, but he gripped

my elbow. I should've known he'd use his no-sex rule to play yet another mind game with me.

"Wait." He glanced up and released a breath. "We're getting side-tracked again. I thought the orgasm might put you in a better mood."

"I wasn't...I don't need you doing me any favors. I can manage on my own just fine." I shoved him out of the way. I didn't need to be pacified.

"Oh? Is that so?"

"You're an asshole." I strode out of the room.

After being in a dim-lit room for so long, the lights in the hallway hurt my eyes. I blinked fast and didn't stop until I was safe in my room. Of course, Rex followed me there too.

"For the record." He slammed the door behind him. "All I wanted tonight was a dinner. But you threw my kind invitation back in my face."

"What?" I braced my hands on my hips. "That wasn't even remotely close to an invitation. It was a rude command. You can't just snap your fingers and expect people to do your bidding."

He shrugged and slowly folded his arms over his chest. Because of course, in his world, all he had to do was wave a hand and things would happen exactly as he said.

"Point taken." He stepped toward me. "Can we start over? I need to talk to you. Jesus Christ, we can't even have a civilized conversation. I've never had to deal with this."

I sat on the bed, feeling drained. The good news was Rex just wanted to talk. He wasn't throwing me out. Wait. What? I dropped my head into my hands. No, the good news would be me going home and taking care of Dad. Or, at the very least, I should be looking for my brothers. They were in danger too.

The mattress dipped, and the warmth of his body enclosed me like a cocoon. "Have dinner with me. Please."

"What do you want from me?"

There was enough ceremony in the rope room that I could pretend I was someone else—someone who lusted over a mafia king, someone who sold six months of her life to save her dad. I told myself that the woman in the mirror wasn't me at all. But sharing a meal and conversation was a different matter. I turned to meet his impossibly blue eyes. Rex and I were not friends.

"There are many things I want from you. But for tonight, I'd like to talk about what Michael asked us to do. I trust you haven't forgotten."

I shot to my feet. "You mean find Massimo and Enzo."

"Yes."

"You know where they are?"

"Yes and no." He reached for my hand and pulled me toward him. "I've been keeping tabs on them. But they're smart. They don't want to be found. I think if we tried, we would make a good team."

"Why in the world did you not lead with that an hour ago?" I glanced down at his fingers playing with mine.

"Probably for the same reason you couldn't agree to a simple meal with me." A smirk pulled at his lips. "Are you ready to do that now?"

"You're intolerable."

"I'll take that as a yes. Be ready in half an hour." He sauntered out of the suite, leaving me utterly confused about our arrangement, the non-sex we had, and now this idea that we could work together to find my brothers.

CHAPTER 18
No Rest for The Wicked

Rex

I shut the door behind me and collapsed against the wall. Caterina Alfera was going to be death of me. How could she pull my strings like that? The more important question was how the fuck was I going to keep my hands off her while we worked together to find her brothers. As much as I wanted her, sex between us could get complicated. And I wasn't ready for that.

I sauntered to my suite next door and headed straight for the shower. Though it would take more than a good scrub to get Caterina's scent off of me. She wasn't wrong when she said we had gone too far. If this had been a session with any of my other partners, I would've ended the relationship. Sex wasn't what I needed from those hours. I needed the escape and the sense that I had control. Even if most of it was contrived, it still worked for me. *It kept me sane.*

But with Caterina, I was afraid the line between desire and rope practice had gotten blurred since she dropped her dress in the boardroom and offered herself to me. I had watched her become the woman she was now for over two years, since before her mother died.

In that time, I had developed feelings for her that up until now I was sure they would dissipate with six months of her in my penthouse. But the more I had of her, the more I wanted her. This was exactly the opposite of what I had promised her mom. I had truly made a mess of things.

I ran the cold water and stepped in. But after a few minutes, the spray did nothing to cool my desire. No matter how hard I tried, my mind played Caterina's spectacular climax on repeat. The raspy tone of her voice when she said my name made me rock hard all over again.

Bracing a hand on the marble tile, I considered my options, which were few. Since Michael had come to see me for help, I had not been able to stop thinking about Caterina and the very real possibility that she would come to live with me. That added up to one thing—I couldn't see myself fucking anyone but her.

I gripped my erection and tugged at the tip. It was either this or barge into Caterina's room and throw our contract out the window. I smiled and stroked a few more times. Knowing that she wouldn't say no to sex with me made my cock steel even more. Jesus fuck, the woman was a beautiful contradiction. I pictured her long neck as she lay on my thigh, panting from want. Her perfect tits had looked so proud bound in layers of jute while she begged for release.

"Caterina."

I pumped harder. As my heart increased the drumming in my chest, I let my brain add the final, and most perfect detail— my name on her lips over and over, while she rubbed her pretty pussy alone in her bed. I shot off onto the wall as an orgasm ripped through me. Stroking a few more times, I waited until the last wave of pleasure wore off and Caterina's green eyes faded into the background of my mind.

"Fuck me," I muttered and finished washing off.

Now that I didn't feel so on edge, I could focus on what I had to do tonight. I needed to find Massimo and Enzo, but for that, I needed to earn Caterina's trust. That whole shitshow from before was proof that neither one of us knew how to communicate with the other. Every time we spoke, it was like a damn game of Chinese whispers.

Smiling at the idiot in the tall vanity mirror, I donned the navy suit I had planned to wear to our dinner before Mary Anne delivered the news that Caterina wasn't joining me. Maybe now that we had both gotten a sort of release, our conversation would go a lot smoother. Highly unlikely, but I had to try. I headed out of the room and straight to her suite. I knocked once. And to my shock, she opened the door immediately, brows knitted.

"I come in peace." I put up my hands in surrender.

"I seriously doubt that." She glanced down at her sheath dress and Prada pumps.

So what if it resembled the hot number she wore the day she came to make a deal with me? Why would that upset her? Probably because everything I did revved her the wrong way.

"You look beautiful." I smiled and then I remembered. Shit.

I purposely did not include under garments for her tonight. Not that I had planned anything. I simply wanted to see her reaction. I wanted her to think of her bare pussy during dinner. I wanted her to think of me. But that was before we called a truce of sorts. Or rather, before I realized I needed to call for one.

"Are you ready?" I motioned toward the landing. "We're eating in."

Lips pursed, she sauntered in front of me. I caught up to her with a couple of long strides and placed my hand on her lower back. Her eyes went up in surprise when I ushered her toward the elevator bay, but other than that, she didn't object, as if she was trying extremely hard not to pick a fight with me.

I had no misplaced illusions that she was doing it for me. To Caterina, family was everything. She was here because she wanted to find her brothers. She was here because she promised Michael.

We rode the elevator car in silence to the rooftop. The city lights were the perfect backdrop for a date with Caterina. If this was such a thing, of course.

"It's beautiful up here." She strolled to the large table set up in the middle of the roof garden.

"Yeah. I had forgotten about that. I don't come up often." This place had been Mom's oasis. "I thought you might enjoy the fresh air." I pulled up the chair next to mine.

"You know it's like almost midnight? Do you ever sleep? Or keep normal business hours?" She blurted out as soon as her heart-shaped ass touched the seat. When her skirt rode up her leg, she froze. No doubt she had remembered she wasn't wearing underwear. Her legs pressed together, and my cock twitched. If that wasn't the definition of irony, I didn't know what would be.

"No rest for the wicked, I guess." I cleared my throat and moved to my seat. "We have work to do."

"So, what's the plan to find my brothers? That's why we're here, right?"

"It is." I waved toward the door to get Mary Anne's attention.

She darted toward us and placed a set of manila folders between us. "Dinner is on the way as well, sir."

"Thank you. We can take it from here."

As soon as she was out of earshot, I flipped open the file and turned it so Caterina could read it. While she busied herself catching up on every piece of information I had collected on her brothers since her mom passed away, the chef came in with our covered plates. I had wanted to keep the meal simple, the way I ate every night.

"Mangia benne." He removed the cover and took off.

"Thank you." Caterina stared at the pan seared Bronzino and roasted vegetables. "I thought you ate caviar and washed it down with the blood of your enemies?"

"That sounds like a recipe for indigestion." I sat back to meet her eyes. "I'm not the beast you think I am."

"No? Just a run of the mill health nut? Huh?" She chuckled, shaking her head at the work of art the chef had prepared for us.

"Ramen noodle packs are not good for you." I motioned for her to eat.

"I love Ramen. Don't knock it 'til you try it. Wait. Is that in my file?" She cocked her head. "You know what? Don't answer that."

"It is." I poured wine into her glass. "You should really cut back on sodium and junk food."

"You should really mind your own business." She inhaled deeply over her meal as she placed a napkin on her lap. "This is my favorite." She took a forkful of the fish, then moaned. "Except better."

"She approves." I took a long sip from my glass. "So, what do you think? I lost track of both your brothers about a month ago. Where should I look next? I let it go before because I hadn't confirmed the FBI was a real threat to us. But now every minute they spend out of my reach, where I can't protect them, they're sitting ducks."

"I can't believe this is happening. Isn't the job of the FBI to put you in jail and call for a fair trial?"

"They like to think so. But this thing with the Society, it has always been sort of personal. I think it started with Dad and Michael. My grandfather used to tell me stories of a time when government officials would come to us for help. We used to maintain the peace out on the streets. We protected our own."

"I know. Dad used to tell me stories too." She offered me a genuine smile.

"We won't let them win. Whatever their reasons for coming after us, whether it's personal or they just want a shiny badge for catching a big whale, the end game is the same. They want us all dead. I can't let them do that."

"Why haven't they come after you?"

"I'm not sure." I shrugged. "They either don't know who I am, or they have something bigger planned. Jesus, I can't even say for sure this is the FBI's doing. I'm running blind here."

"All this killing doesn't make sense. Don't they have laws for that? Maybe an agent gone rogue?" She put down her fork and leaned forward. "If we find my brothers, maybe they can help."

"That's what I'm hoping for. We need a truce so we can combine our resources and figure this out."

The pressure on my chest lifted some. Caterina finally understood the kind of danger we were all in. With Michael's support, and now Vittoria's, we had a shot at getting the son of a bitch who dared come after the families.

We finished our dinner in silence. From the deep V between Caterina's brows, I could tell she was really trying to figure out where she could find her brothers. Her phone had led us nowhere. Even though she had texted them multiple times, they had been smart not to respond. I reached inside the pocket of my suit coat.

"You can have this back." I placed her mobile on the table. "We've added a few security protocols to it. You can use it to call Michael now."

"Thank you." She beamed at me then glanced down at the screen. After a while, her smile faded. No surprise there. Her brothers hadn't reached out. "They're ignoring me. Dad could've died."

"Do you know any of their friends in Ibiza? Anyone who could give us a clue where Massimo took off to? He was there for a long time then disappeared."

"Not really." She sucked in a breath with recognition in her eyes. "Your file didn't say anything about Enzo's yacht, the Lady Anna." Her gaze lowered to her glass. "He named it after Mom. Anyway, he keeps it at Port d'Eivissa."

"We checked with the port authorities, but they said they didn't know anything about them. But of course, Enzo could've paid them off to buy their silence." I grabbed my own phone and texted my security detail. I had sent a crew there a few weeks back to make contact. They should still be there.

Before we had no reason to believe the port authorities would lie to us. But now that we knew Enzo had a connection to the marina there, it would be easy to go back, offer enough motivation, and then ask the right questions. Was it as simple as that? Enzo and Massimo seemingly fell off the face of the Earth because they had been out to sea this whole time?

"If they sailed their boat somewhere near Ibiza, we'll find out soon." I reached for her hand, half-expecting for her to pull back. When she didn't, my heart skipped a beat. Jesus, my fingers itched to reach up her thigh. Would she let me rub her pussy again? *Fuck me.* I shook my head and grabbed the bottle of wine. "You should see the view from the other side. Come on."

When I pulled on her fingers, she stood and followed me to the seating area facing Central Park, which was a stunning sight this time of night. She ambled toward the cinderblock wall with her mouth slightly open.

"If I lived here, I would spend my days in this very spot."

"You're here for the next six months. The place is yours." I handed her a fresh glass of wine. "The roof garden belonged to my mother. Call it a peace offering."

"You've never mentioned her before." She took the globe and drank.

I pursed my lips and shook my head once, a silent request to leave it alone.

"What happens now?"

"We wait for news." I closed the space between us. It was getting harder and harder to keep my hands off her. Especially when she looked at me with so much awe in those gorgeous eyes. "What we do with our time is up to us."

"Rex."

My breath hitched. "Don't say my name unless you mean it." I wrapped my arms around her waist.

"What am I doing here?" She placed her hand inside my jacket, right over my heart.

"I thought the contract was very clear."

"You damn well know what I mean. Why the dinner? Why this view? Why am I here without underwear or a bra?"

"I don't know." I pressed my forehead to hers.

"You just like messing with me, don't you?" She molded her body to mine, pressing her sex on my thigh. The thin fabric of her dress was soaked through. "Admit it."

"I feel alive when I'm with you. When you shoot daggers at me, all I want to do is—"

My Goddamn phone decided to ring just then. It was probably for the best. I tapped on the screen. "You got something, Frank?"

"I do, boss."

I met Caterina's gaze, and she stood at attention. She knew this was about her brothers. Knowing I would probably regret it later, I put the call on speakerphone. "Go ahead."

"Massimo spent the last month on his brother's yacht. But he took a jet back to the States this morning."

"He's coming to New York." Caterina covered her mouth.

"No, he's not. He's headed for Atlanta."

"Atlanta?" We asked in unison. "What the fuck is in Atlanta?"

"Dunno. You need me to set up a team, boss?"

"Yes. We leave in the morning." I hung up the phone and glanced up at Caterina.

Her eyes were wet with tears. Suddenly, she didn't look so defeated as before when she had come to me to save her dad.

Having a brother in town could really throw a wrench in all the plans I had for her.

Caterina had signed a non-disclosure agreement, so I was certain she wouldn't divulge the particulars of our arrangement. The problem was her brothers hated me as much as she did. If they found out she was living with me, they might start a war, which was the last thing I needed with the Feds riding our asses.

So, the one-million-dollar question was—how in the hell was I going to save the Alfera brothers from getting slaughtered, and at the same time, keep Caterina with me? The click clacks of her pumps caught my attention. She was leaving.

"Where are you going?" I darted toward her and gripped her elbow before she reached the elevator.

"To get my things." She yanked at her arm.

"Why?" I towered over her. And just like that, we were back to square one.

"Because I'm coming with you."

"Absolutely not."

CHAPTER 19
My Little Virgin

CATERINA

"You don't get to tell me that I can't go." I stepped back. Not because I was afraid of Rex, but because I needed space, distance to think clearly. "You asked for my help. Remember?"

"I know."

"If it hadn't been for me, you never would've thought to go back to Ibiza and dig deeper."

"I know that too." His shoulders relaxed. "You're so stubborn."

The deep, velvety tone of his voice lulled my senses. When he reached for my cheek, getting away from him didn't even occur to me. This entire day had been surreal. I had spent the better part of it learning about Kinbaku. Then because my life was this side of crazy, I let him tie me up and get me off. The memory of that orgasm washed over me as he skimmed a hand down my lower back. At first, shame flickered in my belly, but then it turned into something else, something like yearning and desire all meshed together.

"I appreciate the help. But we don't know why Massimo is going to Atlanta. We don't know if he's alone or with someone else. We don't know if he's being chased." He brought me closer to him. "The only thing we know for sure is that we're flying blind. I don't want you in the middle of all that. It's too dangerous."

"I get that." I wedged my hand between us. "But you brought me into this, this mafia world of yours. You can't keep me tucked away. It doesn't work that way."

He tilted my chin up to meet my gaze. At first, I thought he was going to kiss me again. The stubborn part of me immediately decided to let him. But when he didn't move, I realized he was trying to sort it all out. Did Rex care about me? He cared what I thought? About my safety?

"I suppose it comes down to this." I inched closer to him. "How badly do you want to find my brother? If he finds out I'm with you, he'll think twice about running off again."

That was a long shot because, technically, Massimo had already left me when I needed him the most. In the last two years, he never reached out to me, not even to see if the pain of losing Mom had killed me already. My eyes watered like they always did when I thought of my broken family. I braced myself for the avalanche of emotions that tended to follow—the sorrow, the self-pity, and all the regret. But Rex held me tighter. He didn't move or try to tell me some cliché line, like time heals all wounds. We both knew it didn't.

"I know it hurts," he whispered after a long while.

"Let me come with you. I promise I'll do anything you say."

He hissed and buried his nose in my hair. "Now that's something I'd like to see happen at least once before I die."

"Is that a yes? You're letting me join your team?" I beamed at him. "Operation: Get Massimo?"

"Yes, I think you're right. Massimo might hear me out, if you're with me." He bent down and pressed his lips to mine.

The act felt so intimate and normal, as if we were a couple, which we weren't. We were just two people playing rope, and now playing detectives.

"Did it ever occur to you that you could, I don't know, call the police?" I meant it as a cute joke. But Rex didn't laugh. Instead, he dropped his hands away from me, knitting his brows.

"If I thought they could help, I would. But the incident with Michael has me questioning everything. For now, we can only trust our own." He glanced down at my dress. "You should get some rest. Tomorrow is going to be a long day."

"Yeah, I should go pack." I started toward the elevator, then stopped to face him. "I have nothing to pack."

He smirked, and I had to bite my tongue not to lash out. After all, he had agreed to let me go with him. He reached into his coat and pulled out his phone. "Mary Anne, Ms. Alfera and I are traveling tomorrow. Could you pack two bags?" He listened to her response, then continued, "Yes, that'll do."

"Thanks." I rolled my eyes. "One day you'll have to tell me what this whole clothes thing is about."

"Yes, I suppose, one day I'll have to." He motioned toward the elevator. "I'll walk you back to your room."

"That won't be necessary."

"No, but it's what I want to do."

His gaze was so full of indecent promises and really bad ideas. I broke away first and headed out. He stayed silent as we rode the car back downstairs and then strolled up the grand staircase. I imagined this was what a date night would be with Rex—stunning views, expensive wine, and dinner with a side of *mobstering*. I had no doubt in my mind that because of me someone thousands of miles away, in Ibiza, got a good beating for lying. And then another round so he would tell the truth about my brother. How was I ever going to date regular men after meeting someone like Rex? And more importantly, why was I not scared out of my wits right now?

We stopped at my door and he pushed it open for me. "Good night, Caterina."

"Good night." I stepped away from him, and he gripped my upper arm.

"No matter what happens tomorrow, I need you to remember our agreement because I have zero intention of letting you go. Your brothers be damned."

"Good night, Rex." I pulled my arm away and shut the door in his face.

What the hell did that mean? That I wasn't allowed to tell my brothers about the contract I signed? I already knew that. For one, I didn't want to break our deal and watch Dad go to jail. But more than anything, I didn't want Enzo and Massimo to know how far Dad had spiraled downward since Mom died. Dad would probably have another heart attack out of shame if my brothers found out about his gambling addiction. Michael Alfera was a proud man. Dad would hate for his sons to see this weaker side of him.

I ambled toward the bed, where Mary Anne had laid out a set of pajamas, underwear included. Shaking my head, I donned the fresh clothes and climbed into bed. Tomorrow, my brother was coming home.

Hours later, I woke up with a startle. I sat up and listened for sounds in the dark room. My phone said it was five in the morning. With my heart beating fast, I threw the covers off me. As soon as my feet hit the floor, Mary Anne stepped out of the ensuite bathroom.

"Jesus, you scared the hell out of me." I pressed a cold hand to my forehead. "Do you ever sleep? What in the world?"

"I'm sorry. Mr. Valentino asked me to make sure you were ready for your trip." She pointed toward the steamy room behind her. "Your bath is ready. I can wait and do your hair."

"Our trip?" Between the scare and my sleepy brain, her words hadn't fully registered. "Omigod, we're flying soon?"

"Yes." She put up her hands. "You have an hour. No rush. All your things are packed and loaded in the car."

I rubbed my face with both hands. My things? What things? "You don't have to stay. I can manage. A bath actually sounds like a good idea. Thanks." I padded to the bathroom and shut the door.

While I got ready, Mary Anne had come in with breakfast. She stood there until I finished the fruit and scrambled eggs— Rex's orders. She then proceeded to rush me into a mini dress with a side long sleeve. The powder blue georgette fabric was soft and very flattering on me, which was a good thing since I didn't have underwear to wear with it.

Just as Rex had said, we pulled out of his private garage exactly an hour later.

Jesus, if it wasn't for the fact that Massimo was waiting for me on the other side of this flight, I would be so annoyed to be hurried like this. It wasn't like we were late to catch a flight. We were flying Rex's Gulfstream. The whole ride to La Guardia, Rex stayed on his phone giving instructions to the different crews. He had stayed in touch with the men in Ibiza.

And now he had people in Atlanta. Did he sleep at all last night? Not that it showed. He looked as he always did—in control, powerful, hot. His wet hair and body wash scent stirred butterflies in my stomach.

He hadn't looked at me at all since we left the penthouse. For some stupid reason, that hurt my feelings. I had gotten so used to his attention and the way he ogled me. Yeah, it was crude and disrespectful. So why the hell was I missing it today? When did I become so addicted to his touch and his ministrations?

As soon as we pulled into the hangar, Rex climbed out and walked around the car to escort me to the plane. He ushered me to the big leather seat in the first row and bent over to help me with the buckle. For the first time this morning, his gaze found mine. The way his fingers lingered over my legs made all my frustration go away.

"The dress suits you."

"Bite me." I pursed my lips.

I meant it as an insult for the way he rushed me out of the house, for ignoring me the whole way here, and for the whole no-underwear thing. But of course, that didn't hurt him in the least. Instead, he smirked at me as if my bad mood amused him.

"Maybe later." He sat across the aisle with a smug smile on his face.

I glared at him, shaking my head. He was fucking messing with me. I opened my mouth to tell him no, but the flight attendant blocked my view. Maybe that was for the best. Rex and I needed to be a team today. All this petty back and forth wasn't helping my cause.

"Can I get you a drink, Rex?" she asked him with her back to me.

Rex? Okay.

"No, I'm good." He reclined on the headrest to find my gaze again.

"How about you, hun? Can I get you a glass of rosé?" The flight attendant shifted to her right to face me, though her body stayed closer to Rex.

Violet called me Hun. It was her own short version of bunny, which I was pretty sure had to do with being a rope bottom. Did everyone on the plane know what I was to Rex? My cheeks flushed. "No, thanks."

I glanced out the window and did my best to ignore Rex's eyes on me. After a while, he reached across the aisle and brushed the back of his forefinger along my forearm. That was all it took for my body to melt into the seat. I squeezed my eyes closed, hating how much Rex could affect my moods.

"I thought the trip would put you in a nicer disposition."

Why was there humor in his voice?

"I'm fine."

"I didn't ask." He cocked an eyebrow, then his gaze shifted toward the front of the plane. He made a gesture with his head that apparently meant "leave us alone" because the two flight attendants disappeared immediately behind the galley curtains. "Come on." He offered me his hand as he stood.

"Where are we going?" My heart raced with anticipation. By now, I recognized that look in his eyes. He couldn't possibly mean to tie me up here with everyone hiding just a few feet away. "No."

"I'm not asking." With a half-smirk pulling at his lips, he gripped my elbow and hoisted me off my seat.

"Do they know? About me? You know." I couldn't even say the words aloud. Did they freaking know I was his rope bottom?

"Do you care what they think?" He cocked his head to look me in the eyes.

"Yeah, I do. She called me hun."

"She calls everyone that."

"Not everyone. She called you Rex."

"Hmm...so that's what this is about?" He released a breath and flashed me a charming smile. "They don't know."

"She was so friendly. I thought maybe she was an ex or something."

"I like this look on you." He gripped my waist and pressed his forehead to mine. "I could have anyone I want, including her. But for some reason beyond my comprehension, it's you I can't stop thinking about. I want you so damn much, it hurts."

"Rex." I took in his scent, and a ribbon of desire coiled itself around my clit. He had no right to look this good in a tailored suit, and then say those things to me.

"I'm right here." He cradled my cheek and slowly stalked toward the suite in the rear of the plane, pulling me with him. "Jesus, you're already wet and ready for me. My little virgin." He nuzzled my neck, then bit me gently.

Somewhere in the back of my mind, a tiny voice told me to refuse and return to my seat. But I didn't listen. His intense look was hypnotizing as he opened the door and ushered me inside the luxurious bedroom. A double bed dotted with gold and navy-blue pillows faced a large, shiny desk on the other side of the cabin. With my heart in my throat, I waited as he ambled toward the table and pulled a coiled rope from the drawer.

"You gotta be kidding me?" I panted a breath. If I had been turned on before, the cord put me over the edge.

"I'm not." He raised a brow, sucking in his bottom lip. His gaze darted between the small, carpeted space in front of me and the mattress. "Let's try the bed."

I shook my head no, but I did as he asked anyway and kneeled on top of the plush comforter, facing the headboard. His hands found my neck and started kneading gently until I relaxed against his chest. The silky-smooth fabric of his coat rubbed against my bare shoulder and sent a flutter across my navel. I was already wet for him. Not that it mattered. This session wasn't about sex. Rex was too cruel to give me that kind of relief. I ached for him to fill me, to put out this fire between my legs.

"Paying for sex doesn't seem like such a bad idea right about now." His lips ghosted the side of my mouth.

His erection pressed against my ass, and a shock of adrenaline rushed through me. Was he seriously considering throwing out his own rule to not pay for sex? Heat rushed to my core and cheeks at the realization that if he tried, I wouldn't say no.

CHAPTER 20
Sitting Ducks

CATERINA

"You're always so tense," he whispered on the column of my neck while he removed his jacket and dress shirt.

"It's kind of difficult to relax around you."

"Take a deep breath and hold it."

By the time he asked me to exhale, his commanding voice was the only thing in my head and my hands were tied in front of me. He picked them up over my head then pulled them toward him so my wrists would cross on the nape of my neck. The effort stretched the top of my dress across my breasts, and my skirt lifted to just below my bare pussy.

"So beautiful." His hot breath traveled down my back as he wound the rope under my boobs and over them.

"What is this called?"

"What?" He stopped to study my profile.

"I know they have names. What's the name of this tie?"

In my peripheral vision, he grinned at me as he slid his fingers down my underarm. "Wakizarashi Shibari because of the exposure of the armpits. In Japanese culture, showing them is considered shameful." He ran his forefinger up to my elbow then planted a soft kiss there. "In English, it's just called a simple bunny tie because your elbows make it look like you have bunny ears."

Bunny, bun, hun. I thought of Violet and her cute name. Oddly enough, though, shame wasn't what I was feeling right about now. Especially not with Rex's hot breath on the nape of my neck, and his deep voice so close to my ear.

"I'm glad you're taking an interest in the study." He brushed his knuckles along the side of my body, all the way to my thigh.

Only Rex would talk about bondage like it was this everyday thing. For crying out loud, we were rope playing thousands of feet off the ground. Rex lived in his own world where time and place didn't matter, where dinners at midnight and flights at dawn were a thing. He tugged at the rope behind me until my head rested on his shoulder. The bed wasn't as firm as a mat. I had to spread my knees farther apart to keep my balance.

In this room, he had no music playing, but he still seemed to move to a certain rhythm as if he could hear a tune in his head. The soft pressure of his hand guided me to double over and rest my chest on my thighs. He climbed on the bed. Every breath of mine was aligned with his measured movements until he sat across from me, legs stretched out on either side of me.

I lifted my torso and got a good look at him. Jesus, the man was beautiful. I wanted to touch all that hot skin over defined abs and chest. When I exhaled, he gripped my waist and brought me closer to him. I landed with my tits in his face, straddling his thigh. The sensation of my throbbing clit against his dress pants was more than I could bear. I let out a moan that if it weren't for the booming hum of the jet engine, I was sure everyone in the cockpit would've heard.

"Shhh." He clamped a hand over my mouth. "I want to see you come."

My eyes widened in surprise. How the hell was I supposed to do that with my arms tied over my head and down my back. I could hardly move or breathe.

"Now, Caterina." His gaze dropped to my bare pussy. The dress had ridden so far up, I could only imagine the view he had of me and my wet folds, grinding on his muscular thigh through the fabric of his pants. But there was nothing I could do to help it. In this position, he controlled my entire body. "We haven't much time." He slid his free hand down to my hip and softly kneaded it.

Shame washed over me when I realized that not only could I come like this, but that I also wanted to. I dug my knees into the mattress and quickly settled into a gyrating pace. I panted into the warm confinement of his palm while he technically forced me to watch him, watch me. The way he looked at me like I was dessert or the last meal on Earth was a huge turn on.

"I'm close." The muffled words didn't sound like me.

He lifted his leg and that was all I needed to get me over the edge. The raw bundle of nerves at the apex of my sex exploded into tiny sparks of fire and burned through me fast. I kept at it, trying to ride every last wave of sensation. It all ended much too quickly, like something was left out of the equation. I met Rex's gaze.

"Soon," he whispered, as if he could read my thoughts,

then reached behind me and unraveled the rope. Gently, he brought my arms down to rest on my lap. I brought my legs together and stayed in his arms like that while he brushed his fingers across my cheek. "We'll be landing in a few minutes. You'll find what you need in the bathroom."

I stretched my legs and let them drop on the side of the bed, feeling cold and confused. "I thought you wanted me."

"I do. But not like this. Not while Michael's debt is hanging over our heads." He rose to his feet and headed to the small closet next to his desk, where he had a fresh suit waiting for him.

And just like that, he was done with me. I strode to the bathroom and shut the door behind me. Tears of frustration rolled down my cheeks. Rex was impossible. I wiped my face and reached for the carry-on bag. Mary Anne had packed toiletries for me, including a mineral water facial spray and underwear. I could only imagine the kind of conversations Rex and she had about me.

"Are you ready?" Rex rapped on the door.

"One second." I made use of the Evian bottle to soothe my puffy eyes and donned the panties. When I opened the door, I felt more like myself. I couldn't let Rex get in my head like that. I had to stay focused on getting my family back together. They were the only reason I was here.

When we landed, the flight attendant opened the plane door and Rex's crew boarded. I turned to Rex with furrowed brows. "We're not leaving?"

"Not yet. I need a full debriefing first and a solid plan."

His private jet basically became a war room of sorts. Rex went back to his business persona. He ignored me while he shook hands with the crew in Atlanta and got the latest update. Except this time, he included me in the conversation to make sure everyone knew I was there to help. It was better, but I still felt like I shouldn't be here, like I was being an imposition.

The day wore on while they finalized their plan and security. I tried not to dwell too much on the fact that we were here hunting my brother. But one thing was for sure, if we were here looking for him, there was a good chance the FBI was too. According to Rex's guy, the Bureau's resources were limitless. After a late lunch in the main cabin, Rex finally decided it was time to head to the hotel and settle in for the night.

Thirty minutes later, we pulled up to the front door of the Four Seasons in Midtown. The executive suite Rex escorted me to was exactly what I thought Rex would go for, a luxury room with a living area, a fireplace, and a butler. According to Frank, we hadn't managed to reserve the whole floor on such short notice, but we did have the entire corridor all to ourselves. Rex seemed satisfied with that answer as he ushered me into what would be our bedroom. We could barely make it through a ninety-minute flight from New York City to Atlanta. I couldn't even imagine what this new setup would mean for us.

"Where are you going to sleep?" I turned to face him after his guys dropped our bags and left.

"Here."

"With me?"

"I'm not letting you out of my sight."

"I can take the couch." I exhaled and inhaled evenly, the way he had shown me during our sessions. Leveling my breathing on my own wasn't as easy without Rex guiding me through it, though.

"You're sleeping on the bed." He deadpanned.

"Well, there's always the terrace."

"I'll think about it." He stalked toward me. "You should get something to eat. The bar downstairs offers a decent menu."

Who had time for food? I opened my mouth to object, but then Frank barged in with a wild look on his face. My heart beat spiked, while I expected the worse. Were we too late? Was Massimo hurt?

"He called in." He stopped in his tracks a few feet from Rex.

"What did he want?"

"A favor." His smile stretched from ear to ear.

This was the best news he could deliver to his boss. If Massimo needed something bad enough to call Rex's crew, then he was in such deep shit, he would be willing to do anything Rex asked. Wasn't that how he got me to become his rope plaything?

"Give him whatever he wants."

"We're on it. And then?" Frank exchanged a meaningful look with Rex. "Where do we take him?"

"Bring him to me." He glanced at me, then shook his head. "On second thought, I'll go to him. Let me know when you have an address for him."

Frank nodded then left in a hurry. As soon as the door shut behind him, the air shifted. It was lighter and less murderous. I didn't want to think that Rex would order my brother's execution just because he refused to do what we needed him to do. I shook my head to clear my thoughts. Rex wasn't that guy. He would never do that to his own family. That much I knew for certain about him—Rex thought of everyone in the Society as his family.

"What happens now?" I sat on the upholstered chair by the balcony.

Now that the immediate danger was over, I was able to take the time and take in the room. The entire decor was centered around plush and elegance. All done in creams, yellows, and powder blues.

"We wait for Massimo to make his next move." Rex ambled over to me and sat on the four-poster bed across from me.

The act was so intimate and friendly, I didn't know how to respond. Mainly, because the last time Rex and I had a few hours to kill, it ended with me riding his leg until I came. Fuck. I needed to stop thinking about that and focus.

"Too bad I already used up my hour for the day." He smiled at me, then glanced down at his phone. His shoulders stiffened instantly.

"What is it?" I shot to my feet.

"Nothing." He shook his head.

"I thought you said you didn't lie."

"Fine." He blew out a breath while his gaze darted from his bags to me. "I'm sorry." He picked up his suitcase and plopped it on the mattress.

"Sorry about what? What's going on with Massimo?" I leaned on the footboard with my heart thrashing in my ears. "We're a team, remember? You can tell me. I'm not some fragile flower."

He placed a hand over mine and met my gaze. In the next beat, the cold steel of his handcuffs hit my wrists with a sharp flick. "Sorry about this. But we're flying blind here. I can't let you come with us. Not yet."

"Where are you going?"

"Massimo had dinner at the St. Regis, about four miles from here. Sounds like he left in a hurry before he even finished his meal. Shortly after that, he called Vittoria asking for a favor to help a woman. Vittoria just sent me the details."

"You're going there now?"

"Yes. Turns out he's staying there too."

"You're gonna ambush him when he comes home?" I yanked at the chains, scowling at him. "I can talk to him. Let me come with you."

"No." He put up his hands as if he meant me no harm and shuffled away from me. "As soon as it's safe, I'll come for you."

"For the record, this is why I don't trust you," I called after him.

He paused at the door for a moment, but then took off. Damn him.

I got that the FBI had put a target on our backs. But shackling me to a post was overkill. It wasn't like the feds were in a hurry to make a huge scene at a luxury hotel this far from New York City. Massimo didn't trust Rex. The second he got wind Rex was on his tail, he was going to disappear again. Massimo was ignoring my calls, but I was sure he wouldn't turn me down in person. We were family.

If Rex thought I would stay here like some puppy and wait for him to return with news, he had another thing coming. I glanced around the room for a way out. The room phone was on the other side of the bed. I winced at the idea of having to explain my predicament to the concierge. It wasn't like I could lie about it. What could I possibly say that wasn't utterly mortifying?

"Hello?" I shouted at the shut door. "Anyone there?"

When I didn't get a response, I plopped myself on the bed

and dropped my head into my free hand. No doubt Rex left a whole team right outside my door. So even if I could get the cuffs off, I would still need to deal with them.

The minutes ticked by while I stared at the empty suite. Then it hit me. Rex had to have a key somewhere in here as a safety precaution. Wasn't that why he always had rope shears within reach when he tied me up? I grabbed his bag and dumped the contents on the comforter, then rummaged through all the small pockets. Sure enough, he had the keys in there. No doubt he did that on purpose. He didn't mean to keep me chained to the bed all night. Just long enough so he could go after my brother. The pressure on my chest lifted as I made quick work of the lock to free myself.

I darted to my bag sitting on the sofa and fished out my phone. How long ago had Rex left? Maybe an hour? If I called a car service now, I might still get to Massimo in time. Wishing I was wearing better clothes for this mission, I tiptoed to the door and pressed my ear to it. The commotion on the other side sent my pulse into overdrive—several men were talking fast and at the same time, I couldn't really make anything out. Something was wrong.

Did the FBI send someone after me again?

I listened harder as a table got knocked over, and Frank called for help. The fear in his tone compelled me to swing the door open and rush into the living room, just in time to see Rex, the invincible king, fall to his knees in the middle of the foyer.

"What the hell happened?" I kneeled next to Rex, ready to catch him, though I knew that if he passed out on me, I wouldn't be able to hold him.

"Long story." Frank appeared in my line of sight with a medical kit. "He got shot."

Adrenaline rushed through me as I took inventory of the amount of blood on his suit coat and dripping down his fingers. Rex couldn't die like this. I fisted my hands to warm them up and exhaled. This wasn't the time to lose my shit. "We need to call an ambulance."

"No hospital," Rex mumbled, "I'll be a sitting duck."

"Okay. Um. Let's bring him into the bedroom. He can't stay on the floor."

Rex needed a doctor. Where the hell were we going to get one? If we were in New York, we'd have access to his own network of people, but out here in Atlanta, we were, as he'd said, sitting ducks.

CHAPTER 21
Mobsters or Doctors?

Rex

Fuck me. Between the sleepless night, the flight here, and the altercation with what I was certain was an FBI agent gone rogue, I was starting to think my luck had run out. The searing pain in my shoulder kept me lucid, but I had lost too much blood on the way to the hotel. Ironically, the face-off had happened at a hospital nearby, but it was like I had said, without the proper contacts, I couldn't risk letting one of the doctors treat me. They were required to report all gunshot wounds. The FBI would take all of two seconds to connect the dots and find their way to me.

"Bed sounds like a good idea." I let Frank hoist me up and half-carry me to the bedroom where Caterina had already tossed all the bedding aside and covered the mattress with bath towels.

"Why are you smiling?" She shoved a strand of hair away from her face and reached for my suit jacket.

"You're worried about me." I winced while she removed my clothes, including my pants, shoes, and socks. Not how I had envisioned our night would go.

"I'm worried my brother did this to you." Her eyes softened. "Did he? Did Massimo shoot you?"

"No." I sat on the edge of the bed, angling my neck to check the wound. "Looks like my luck hasn't quite left me yet."

"Your shoulder is split open. How is this good news?" She wedged herself between my thighs and pressed a clean kitchen towel to the area. "I think you're supposed to keep pressure on it until it stops bleeding. Or at least, that's what I've heard, I don't even know if that's true." Her lip trembled.

The deep V between her brows told me she cared more about my well-being than keeping her distance. She hovered her fingers near the gash then took the hydrogen peroxide from Frank and squirted it all over my left side.

"Fuck." The burn intensified as froth built around the injury. When the room swayed a few rounds, I squeezed my eyes shut.

To my surprise, Caterina cradled my cheek and spoke in a gentle tone I had only heard her use with Michael. "You should've let me come with you."

"And risk you being the one sitting here, wounded? Absolutely not." I swallowed against the pain. "How is it?"

"It looks like the bullet went through your muscle." She squinted while she assessed the damage. "He's going to need stitches. A lot of them," she said to Frank.

"Everything you need should be in the medical kit." He presented the bag like it was a peace offering of sorts. "I have sausages for fingers. I can't." Frank put up his arms as proof.

Next to Caterina's delicate features, his hands looked like dust pans.

"So, I have smaller appendages and automatically I'm supposed to know how to sew?" Her gaze darted between Frank's and mine. "I don't like needles."

"No, but if I have the choice, I'd rather have a delicate touch tending to my wounds." I reached for her wrist and kissed the inside of it. "I trust you. The sooner you patch me up, the sooner we can go home."

"We can go home." She echoed my words, pressing a hand to her forehead. "Fine. I need to call Sam first. You stand a better chance if someone walks me through it."

"That's a good idea." I lay down on the pillow. The soft bed felt good, and suddenly my body weighed a ton.

"I got it." Frank stepped away as he reached into the pocket of his trousers.

"This is the craziest thing I have ever done." Caterina cleared the bedside table and dumped all the contents of the first aid kit onto it. "This is why Mom refused to be part of this mafia world. She hated the idea of Dad coming home bleeding like this." She waved a hand toward me.

"You're mumbling." I reached for her waist and got her to sit next to me. "I'm fine. I just need a few sutures and a shot of whiskey."

"Tell me the truth. Did my brother...?" She trailed off.

"No, he didn't. Massimo and I had a relatively civilized conversation. He's not happy, but he's willing to come home. He was with Mikey Gallo."

"Gallo? I thought the entire family had been wiped out."

"We thought so too. Massimo has been hiding him this

whole time. But now because of Gallo, they, the feds, or whoever tried to kill us tonight, also know about Massimo."

"What do you mean?"

"Gallo wanted to start a street racing business here in Atlanta. Long story short, the locals didn't like it. He retaliated by kidnapping one of their own. Massimo and I went to Mikey to talk some sense into him and ended up getting mixed up in a shoot-out. I got a good look at one of the guys. He smelled like a pig."

"You think he was FBI?"

"He had that look in his eyes." I nodded.

"Where's Massimo? Is he okay?"

"He is. He said he had something he needed to handle first, but that he would meet us in New York." I blinked slowly to chase the shadows creeping on the edges of my eyes. "I trust him. You'll see your brother soon. Once he's home. He'll be safe. I promise."

Tears spilled down her pink cheeks. "Thank you."

Frank came back with Nurse Sam on the phone. "He wants to see your arm."

I nodded and scooted up the bed to let them do their thing. Caterina jumped to her feet and grabbed the device from Frank. If she was still afraid for my life, she didn't show it. She talked fast as she explained in detail how bad the injury was. Apparently, a mild infection had already settled in. Sam walked her through the process of checking for bone damage, and to see if the lacerations and skin tags were clear of debris before she started sewing me back up.

While she listened intently to Sam's instructions, Frank left the room, then returned with a bottle of Bourbon. He poured three shots and offered one to Caterina. "Nothing can hurt at this point." He shrugged.

"You're right." She took the glass from him and knocked it back. Wincing, she covered her mouth. After she recovered from the lingering burn of the liquor, she shook her hands out and turned to me. "Okay, keep adding pressure. I think I can do this. But I need to practice a few times."

"There's peaches in the kitchen." Frank refilled my empty tumbler. "I'll get them."

"Let me see." She removed the cloth from my shoulder to take a look. "How do people do this for a living?"

"You mean mobsters or doctors?"

"I guess both." She knitted her brows, angling her head one way and then the other to get a better view.

"At home, Sam would've handled this."

"She can do it." Sam's voice boomed from the bedside table.

Frank returned with three choices of fruit for Caterina. My fingers had already gone numb from the aching pain, but watching Caterina practice her stabbing motions on an orange and then a peach kept my mind off the fucked-up situation we were in. I smiled at her profile, noting how she sucked on her bottom lip every time she delivered a measured blow.

"Are you ready?" She glanced up at me from her mangled fruit.

"You're the one doing all the work." I relaxed my body and focused on her scent while she rinsed the affected area again.

The first stitch hurt like a mother fucker, but as she went along, her touch became more assured and precise. At some point, the whole thing became a series of tiny burns. Some areas felt so hot, I didn't even feel the piercing of the needle.

Either the pain was manageable now, or the Bourbon had already kicked in.

"Stay with me," she said urgently. "He's burning up."

In the background, a cacophony of loud voices and phones ringing turned into a deafening echo in my head until Caterina's call for me became a faraway dream. My eyes fluttered closed. The desperate clanking in the room ceased, along with the bright lights, Caterina's touch, and the pain—right before I passed out.

The next morning, I woke up feeling like I had been hit by a truck. Most of my aches and pains wore off the minute I noticed Caterina curled up next to me. She had changed into pajamas shorts and a tank top and her hair was up in a ponytail. Her form looked so small and delicate next to me. I wanted nothing more than to pick her up and kiss her until she begged me to take her.

My cock steeled under my boxer briefs. Fuck me. If I hadn't gotten shot last night, I might've spent the night buried deep inside her—our contract, her dad, and brothers be damned. Why did she stay with me? Any one of my guys could've slept on the couch to keep an eye on me. Playing doctor was definitely not part of our agreement.

A low moan escaped her lips as she stirred next to me. I could only hope her dreams were just as haunted as mine. Every night, I thought of nothing and no one else but her. I outlined the curve of her hip with my forefinger, remembering how soft her skin was there when she let me touch her on the plane ride here. My gaze settled on the bow of her mouth. God how I wanted to fuck that mouth. I had been so close to doing just that yesterday before I realized we were due to land in a few minutes.

When she nuzzled her face against me, I hovered my fingers over hers and watched her while she stretched her legs out and ran her hands all over my abs and chest. Her puffy eyes and lips made her look so young and so innocent. I took in her flowery scent and the warmth of her body flushed against mine.

Over the years, I had learned so much about Caterina Alfera—everything from her grades in college or her favorite wine, to how many strokes of my rope it took to make her come. But I had no idea what she looked like in the morning after she woke up. Yeah, I could get used to this kind of bliss with her. In the next breath, she sat up with a wild look in her eyes.

"Oh, um, I'm so sorry. I fell asleep." She scooted away from me.

"Don't be. You look good in my bed." I reached for her but caught only empty sheets.

Her gaze dropped to the bulge in my underwear, and her brows shot up in surprise. "You're unbelievable."

"I never said I was a saint. Anyone waking up to a beautiful woman sleeping next to him would've had the same reaction."

"You almost died."

"It was just a scratch."

"You passed out from it. The fever spiked so fast and so high, we had to pump you full of antibiotics."

"I don't understand. Are you mad at me because I find you irresistible or because I almost died?"

"You scared me." She inched closer to me.

"Thank you for helping me. You know you didn't have to. Most people would've left their enemy to die. Why didn't you?

This could've been your way out." My chest tightened at the idea that maybe Caterina Alfera didn't hate me after all. I wanted to hear her say the words—I don't hate you. "I thought you hated me."

She relaxed against the pillows next to mine, suddenly intrigued by her palm lines. Like last night, she gently nibbled on her bottom lip, as if the answer to my question required serious effort.

"I thought I did too." She glanced up at me with tears brimming her eyes. "I don't hate you, Rex."

"Hey." I pulled her toward me until she rested her head on my chest.

"How do you feel?" She pointed her chin at my poorly bandaged arm. "I'm so sorry about all this."

"I'm fine. You never have to worry about me." I buried my fingers in her hair, wishing we were back in my penthouse.

"I was afraid I'd never see you again." She brushed her finger over my brows. "Or talk to you." She panted a breath, and the green in her eyes darkened.

Jesus, I knew that look. She hoisted herself up and kissed me on the lips, soft and tentative at first. But when I cradled the nape of her neck, she completely let her guard down. She thrusted her tongue past my teeth, rubbing those gorgeous tits all over me.

"Fuck." I groaned.

"Did I hurt you?" She pulled away to look at me. Her cheeks burned a bright red, and her eyes showed the level of surprise I had felt at her sudden display of affection.

"God, no." I gripped her waist with my good hand. "You've never kissed me before."

"Yes, I have." She brought her knees in and settled against my side.

"You've kissed me back, but never..." I swiped the pad of my thumb over her lips. "Never this."

Our gazes locked.

Well, who needs a convoluted plan when you have blind luck?

I had been trying to get close to Caterina for years, but the hate she had for my family was too great and she couldn't see past who I was—a beast, she'd called me once. "After all this time, you're telling me that all I had to do to gain your favor was get shot?"

"This isn't that." She climbed out of the bed.

I made to get up, but pain shot up my arm like wildfire. "Jesus." I fell back on the pillow. "Don't go."

She stood in the middle of the room, as if weighing her options. The worry and agony I had seen in her eyes last night was back. A knock on the door saved her from having to make a choice. Blowing out a breath, she fixed her tank top and pajama pants and swung the door open.

"Sorry to bother you." Frank's voice boomed across the room. "Is he up? It's about Massimo."

"Come in," I called and threw the covers over my boxer briefs. Not for me, but I figured Caterina wouldn't want my guys knowing our business. "What is it?"

"Massimo couldn't find Mikey. But he's headed for New York in a few hours."

"There's nothing keeping us here anymore. Get the plane ready. I'd like to go home."

"You got it, boss." He gave me and Caterina a quick nod and took off.

"We're going home?" Caterina padded over to me.

I nodded.

The word on her lips sent a shock through me. She'd said we. Gunshot wound aside, our trip to Atlanta had been more or less a success—Mikey Gallo was still alive. Massimo had agreed to return to the fold, and more importantly, Caterina no longer considered me her enemy. More than that, I believed she cared about me.

CHAPTER 22
You Don't Even Know Me

CATERINA

The flight home turned out to be a whirlwind of getting rushed from one place to another. For whatever reason, Rex wanted to keep his injury a secret. We didn't check out of the hotel. Frank found a private charter plane to fly us out of a smaller airport in Atlanta straight into Teterboro. He even left a few of the guys behind to keep up the charade that he was staying in Atlanta for a couple of weeks, which was the minimum amount of time Sam had said Rex would need to recover.

As soon as we landed, Frank and his team rushed Rex to an ambulance, while I was escorted to an SUV. A tight pressure gripped my chest as my car pulled away, leaving a convalescing Rex behind. He had seemed fine earlier this morning when we kissed. But after all this cloak and dagger, I couldn't help but feel like maybe something was wrong, that I had messed up the sutures somehow.

My driver made record time to Rex's penthouse. When he

pulled up to the private entrance, I didn't wait for him to open the door for me. I climbed out and darted toward the elevator bay. Of course, they knew I was coming. The minute I reached the end of the lobby, a guard appeared to escort me upstairs.

The penthouse was a madhouse. And it was just then when I realized what a huge deal Rex's incident had been. He was the head of the Society. No one was allowed to move a finger unless they had his approval first. As much as the families didn't agree on things, they all conceded that Rex was in charge. If something happened to him, who would take over? I had been so afraid for his life for my own selfish reasons, I hadn't considered what his death would mean for everyone else. What a sad existence, if he couldn't even show a little bit of weakness, not even after getting shot.

I darted up the grand staircase. Out in the hallway, a bunch of people in white coats seemed to be having some sort of conference. I adjusted my gait and slowly made my way toward them. A woman in a tight ballerina bun that reminded me of a much younger version of Signoria Vittoria broke away from the group, waving a hand to get my attention.

"Hi, I'm Dr. Salvatore. I assume you're Caterina?" She offered me her hand, and I shook it. So, she and Vittoria Salvatore were related. I supposed it paid to have a medical doctor in the family. There was so much I didn't know about Rex's world—our world.

"I am." I opened my mouth to ask how he was, but the words didn't come out.

"He's fine. All this is routine to make sure he doesn't lose a limb over this." She cocked an eyebrow. "You did a decent job. He'll have a scar, but hey, at least he gets to keep the pretty face." She laughed at her own joke.

"Yeah, I guess. Can I see him?"

"Maybe later. Right now, he needs to rest. You do too." She stepped closer to look into my eyes.

"I'm fine." I blinked several times to regain focus. "I'll just wait in my..." Shit. I couldn't tell her I was staying in the room next door. Would she know that meant I was Rex's latest resident bottom? "I'll wait in the kitchen."

I turned to leave, but she stopped me. "Caterina, wait." The amusement in her voice pissed me off. She knew. She fucking knew.

"Everyone here is here because Rex trusts them." She pointed at my door. "Get some rest. I'll let Rex know you're home."

I swallowed my pride. One, because I was extremely tired. And two, because it shouldn't matter what Dr. Salvatore thought of me. Though I did hate that she knew so much about me and I knew nothing about her. Why did Rex tell her about me?

"Okay." I strode to my suite with as much dignity as I could muster, locked the door behind me, and face planted on my bed.

The next morning, I woke up to Mary Anne drawing a bath for me. Of course she had a key. I rolled my eyes at her back. "Good morning," I called out.

"Good morning." She smiled. "Welcome home. I brought you some breakfast and fresh clothes."

"Thanks."

Right. I had forgotten this wasn't really home. If it were, I would have my things with me and the key to my own lock. A swirl of bitterness settled in my stomach. I let it stew until I was ready to admit that the real reason I was annoyed with Mary Anne was because I wasn't allowed to see Rex.

"How is he?" I asked on my way to the bathroom.

"Better. He wants to see you."

"Oh." Those five little words shouldn't have made me so happy. "I'll get ready."

I showered and blow-dried my hair as quickly as I could then donned the romper Mary Anne had laid out on the bed before she left. The soft blue and mint green fabric clung to me like a second skin. It was flirty and comfortable and kind of perfect. I ate my breakfast, feeling nervous about seeing him again.

Yesterday, we had left things at a really awkward standoff. Mainly because I wasn't sure what I wanted from Rex. Yeah, sure, every time he was near, I wanted him in my bed. But apart from a physical relationship, I knew there couldn't be more. So, what the hell was I doing here?

I finished my coffee, and after a few calming breaths, I strode over to Rex's room. My heart beat fast against my ribs. And why did this even mean anything to me right now? I was just here to make sure he was fine. As any decent person would do. I rapped on the door and stepped back.

The door swung open, and the stupid grin on my face froze at a weird angle. I bet Dr. Salvatore thought it was terrifying. "Good morning." I used my business voice. "I stopped by to see how the patient was doing."

"He's sleeping," she whispered. "Maybe come back later."

"Oh. Of course. Later." I nodded several times like an idiot. This woman, like Signoria Vittoria, intimidated me. Something about her screamed power and danger. And it was so obvious she didn't like me. Or maybe she just didn't like me near Rex. Did she have a thing for him? I mean, who would blame her?

"She can come in, Donata." Rex's voice boomed inside.

"Come in." She waved me in.

I did my best to keep my gait even and not rush to Rex's California king-size bed on the far end, overlooking the terrace. Rex's suite was as big as my apartment, with a spectacular view of Central Park. The fireplace in the middle of the room made the space seem inviting and calming. Just like downstairs, the color palette followed the same tones of navy blue, grays and browns.

He sat on his bed wearing nothing but sweatpants. His wet hair smelled of body wash as if he had just taken a shower. A pang of jealousy ripped through me before I could stop it. Did Donata help him with that? I shook my head and forced all the sexy images out of my mind. Rex wasn't mine. We weren't even sleeping together.

"How are you?" My voice was barely audible over his fast and furious typing. After a few seconds, he stopped and closed his laptop.

"Good as new." He beamed at me.

"He still needs more days of rest." Donata walked past me and sat at the foot of the bed.

"Your bandages look way better." I pointed at his chest. When I had tried it before I couldn't exactly get the wrap to comfortably go over his shoulder and around his chest, so I coiled it around his arm. Sam had said that it just had to be tight, not pretty. "I um—"

He raised his hand to me then turned to the goddess sitting at his feet. "Donata, can you give us a minute?"

"Of course, dear. Text me if you need anything." She stood

and offered me a smile. "No strenuous exercise for at least a week."

"Okay." I watched her leave and slowly shut the door behind her.

"Come here." Rex offered me his hand.

My body started moving toward him before I could mentally react to his command. I stopped and glared at him. "Is she Vittoria's niece?"

"She is. How did you know?"

"The last name. Is she the niece that's going to be devasted?"

He chuckled. "What do you mean?"

"Vittoria said that when she met me. That her niece was going to be devasted because I was here." What did it matter?

"Come here. Don't make me ask again. We're past all this pretense, aren't we?" His tone was low and layered with sinful promises. "I've been dying to kiss you all day." His extended fingers were like a magnet to mine.

I slid my hand into his and let him pull me on top of him. With our bodies fused together, he kissed me hard until I melted into him. This was always the thing with Rex. He made me throw logic out the window and forget how cold and lonely this place was without him. He made me forget about the gunshot wound I had sewn, but more importantly, he made me forget about Donata.

"Jesus Christ. You have no idea how much I want you."

"I kind of do." I pressed my hips to his massive erection, running my hand up his chest and into his hair. The wet strands brought up images of Rex and Donata in the shower together. "Rex, stop." I muttered, hoping he didn't hear the hitch in my voice.

"What is it?" His eyes searched mine.

"Did she help you with your shower?" I gritted my teeth to stop myself from saying more. That was something a jealous girlfriend would ask, and I was neither.

"No. Why would you think that?" He laughed.

"I'm glad I amuse you." I made to get away from him, but he held me tight. Even in this state, he was still in control. He still held all the power.

"Donata is just one of my doctors and a friend. Nothing more. I promise, I managed the shower all by myself." A sexy grin pulled at his lips. "Maybe you can help me with that tomorrow." He inched his hand from my waist up into the side of my breast.

"Does she know about me?"

He blew out air and that was all the answer I needed.

"I can't believe you. You make me sign a NDA and then you turn around and tell everyone that I'm your plaything." That speech would have been more effective if I was standing on my own two legs and not rubbing myself all over his abs. "I can't keep doing this. It's humiliating."

The smile faded from his face and he loosened his grip on me. "Apart from Violet, who graciously agreed to help guide you through the process, no one knows you're my rope bottom. Those sessions are between you and me and no one else. Do you understand?"

"She knew I was sleeping next door." I raised my voice to make my point.

"She does know about that."

"Why did you tell her?"

"I didn't. Her aunt did." He glanced upward, as if searching for the right words. At this point, there wasn't much he could say to put out this anger I felt in the pit of my belly. "She also told her about how I feel about you."

"Well, that's nothing new. Everyone knows how you hate my family." I sat on the mattress next to him.

A cold shiver ran down my spine when he didn't try to keep me close to him. When I met his gaze, the intense and oh so intimidating fire I found there shocked me out of my moment of insanity. What was I thinking? That I could just climb into bed with Rex Valentino and then what? How was I going to explain to Dad that I slept with his enemy? What would people like Donata and Vittoria think? They belonged here. They understood Rex's world because it was theirs too.

"Last night, I thought we had agreed to stop pretending. I thought you understood." He twisted his body to face me and winced.

"Don't move. You'll hurt yourself." I braced my hand on his chest, so he'd lie down again.

He did, but then brought my lips to his again and kissed me with a hunger that left me breathless. "How is it that everyone can see how I feel about you, except you? All this time. Don't you get it? I want you. It's more than that." He furrowed his brows, staring at me with pursed lips, as if the thing he needed to say next hurt him as much as the gunshot wound on his shoulder. "I love you."

"Violet said you couldn't love. That your heart didn't work that way."

"Now you know why. It's because of you. It's always been you."

My lips parted. How was this even possible? "You don't even know me."

"I know enough. And I've known it for a long time." He

kept his bandaged arm to his side while his fingers massaged the nape of my neck. "Yesterday, I was too high on meds and too much in pain to finish our conversation."

"Rex."

"Let me finish. I know you want me. That much has always been clear to me. What I didn't know was if you could ever stop hating me for just one minute, just long enough to see the real me. To see the man, and not the ruthless king." He puffed out a breath. "Last night, you said you didn't hate me."

I stared at his beautiful face and the softness in his eyes. I thought of our sessions, his gentle touch, and how much I craved him. No one could kiss like that unless they actually felt something. No one could kiss back, unless...

"Say something."

"I don't hate you."

"I know." He pulled me toward him until our foreheads touched. "I'm not asking you to love me."

"What are you asking then?"

His phone rang just then, and he cursed under his breath. Yeah, that was the worst possible timing. Rex Valentino had just confessed the mother of all confessions. The last thing we needed was someone barging in again. He picked up the device and sent the call away. Three seconds later, the screen lit up with a text.

Mary Anne: The Alfera brothers are here. And they're demanding to see their sister.

"Fuck me." He gripped the mobile in his hand.

In an instant, he became the ruthless king everyone feared. The one who never bothered to ask and simply took. This time, I was that something or someone. Massimo and Enzo were probably thinking that same thing. That I was here against my will, which I wasn't. Rex and I made a deal. At first, I had thought he only meant to humiliate me, but I was wrong. He never did anything to bring me shame. Heat rose to my cheeks when I thought about all the times he had made me come because I begged him to. That was all on me.

Rex *loved* me.

My eyes traveled down from his face to my arm, where I was sure his fingers would leave a mark. "My brothers are here?" I pushed away from him, but he held me tighter with both hands this time. "You're staying right here."

"I have to see them. Rex, they've been gone for two years." I struggled until my arms ached under his iron grip.

"No."

"Why not?"

"Because they won't understand what we have."

CHAPTER 23
We Don't Need to Be Out of Time

Rex

"Rex." Her gorgeous lips found mine again.

I had finally told her the truth, and she hadn't taken off. She hadn't said I was out of my mind for thinking she could love me, for thinking she could love a beast. Why couldn't her brothers have waited one more night before they decided they wanted to play the heroes. They left Caterina all alone. All this time, she'd had to deal with Michael on her own. Now they show up thinking they can take her away from me. Not bloody likely.

"You can't keep me from seeing my brothers." She rubbed her nose against mine, letting her body be heavy on top of mine. "Do you hear how insane that sounds?"

"I'm crazy for you." I sucked on the column of her neck until bit by bit, the pieces fell into place and my brain caught on to the fact that she was right. Sooner or later, she had to see Enzo and Massimo. Honestly, I had hoped for later, much, much later. I nibbled farther down to her chest until a button blocked my path. "Do you remember the day you came to see me?"

"Hmmm."

"Your tits have haunted me every night since then."

"I offered myself to you. Technically, served myself up on a platter for you." She let her head fall back. "Why did you refuse me?"

"An irrational sense of duty?" My lips curved over the silky fabric of her romper and her hardened nipples.

"I thought maybe I wasn't your type."

"You're so fucking beautiful. That would be impossible." I kissed across to her other breast, mentally kicking myself for not choosing something for her to wear that showed more cleavage. Earlier, I figured a long sleeve romper would be the safest thing for the type of conversation we had pending for today. "Take it off. Take it all off. I want to see you naked like that day." The commanding tone in my voice made her shiver in my arms. "I bet you're ready for me too. Wet and tight. My little virgin," I whispered in her ear.

"You can't keep doing this to me." She pulled back, panting a breath. "You make everything so fuzzy and tingly and so fucking good."

"Then stay."

"Gosh, you have the worst timing ever. Of everyone I have ever met."

"Seems we're always running out of time." I let my head fall back on the pillow.

"Our deal is our deal." She smiled at me, running her fingers over the fabric to right her clothes. "I'm a woman of my word. I'm staying with you. Massimo and Enzo don't need to get involved. Beyond breathing life back into Dad by just being here, that is. He'll be so happy to see them." She kicked her legs over the side of the bed and padded around to say goodbye.

If she thought I was going to let her go by herself, she didn't know me at all. I exhaled all the air out of my lungs until it burned. Then I inhaled, hoping to find the physical strength for what I had to do next—take Caterina downstairs and somehow not lose her forever.

My phone went off again. I picked up this time. "Tell them we're on our way. And get Frank." I dropped my device in the pocket of my pants.

"You can't walk like this."

"You wanted to see your brothers. Let's go."

I grabbed my T-shirt off the upholstered chair facing the fireplace. For a second, I considered not wearing it just to spite them, to throw them off their game. But then decided against it. When it came to Caterina, I wanted to do things right. Not to mention, it would be better if they didn't find out about my incident in Atlanta. Slowly, I sat on the couch and put on my shoes. Of all the days to only have one good arm, why did it have to be today? Caterina tried to help me, but I waved her away.

"It's okay to ask for help."

I stopped halfway to glance up at her. "You don't think I know that? Why do you think I wanted to see Massimo this week?"

"I was talking about the shoes, but okay."

"I'm sorry." I rose to my feet. "I promise. It may not look like it, but I am trying to do the right thing."

She cradled my neck. "If it weren't for you, I'd be a mess right about now."

"Why do you care what they think?"

"They're my family."

I bit my tongue and decided not to point out the fact that Enzo and Massimo weren't here for her. Michael was up to something. Why else would he send his sons here to retrieve Caterina when he was the one who orchestrated this whole plan? Somehow, I knew that whatever he was scheming, she'd be caught in the middle of it again. Whatever it was, the old man wasn't going to get away with it.

I reached for her hand and pulled her closer to me. I hadn't meant to do much else, but my mouth found hers and I couldn't stop tasting her. Especially after she hung from my neck and deepened the kiss.

"Relax. This is your family. You owe them nothing."

"I know. I just haven't seen them since Mom. And now they're here of all places because of me." She sighed.

"You mean, in their enemy's lair?"

"Don't make fun of me." She slapped my chest, then covered her mouth. "I'm sorry."

"Breathe, Caterina." I turned her around and pressed my lips to her ear, the way I had done our first time in the rope room. "Take a big gulp of air. Fill up. And hold it."

She did as I asked without question. We'd come so far in this regard. I held her for a few more counts and then exhaled along with her.

"Thanks." She smiled at me. "Mom would be so sad to see how disconnected from each other we had become. This isn't us. We're a family. I missed having a family."

The pink had returned to her pretty cheeks and she seemed more in control. She cared about what they thought of her, and that made my insides twist with guilt. If she hadn't been concerned about her dad, she wouldn't be here with me. I wanted to say I was sorry for the deceit. But I knew she wouldn't understand. Not yet. Goddammit, we needed more time.

From the top of the stairs, I spied Enzo and Massimo near the fireplace. Tall and dark was how anyone would describe the brothers. If Caterina was an angel lost in my world, the Alfera brothers were quite the opposite. Because unlike Caterina and her mother, Anna, Michael and his sons never left the Society, not really. For Anna's sake, they all pretended and lied.

"Massimo." Caterina practically ran into her brother's arms.

I let them have their moment while I texted Frank and asked him to be ready. He promptly responded to let me know he had twenty men just outside the front door and another crew downstairs. Unless Enzo was ready for a war, Caterina wasn't going anywhere tonight.

"Are you okay? You look...older." He furrowed his dark brows as he inspected his little sister.

"It's been two years, you asshole." She hit him square in the chest.

I would've gone with a right hook.

Enzo and Massimo towered over her by at least seven inches, same as me. But just how she had never been intimidated by me, she didn't take shit from them either. She gave them an earful on how selfish they had been for taking off and then ignoring all her calls.

"I know." Enzo cut her off in the middle of her speech to pull her into a bear hug. "We were idiots. We messed up.

That's why we're here. We're taking you home. You don't owe him anything."

"It's good to see you boys." I crossed my arms over my chest and immediately regretted it as the pain shot through me.

Enzo glared at me. If they weren't trying to take Caterina away from me, I would've laughed at how familiar that scowl now was to me. Enzo and I were friends a long time ago. Before our parents dropped a bomb on us with their bullshit talk about duty, honor, and doing right by our families. They turned our lives upside down that day. After that night, Enzo and I slowly began to drift apart until our friendship became nothing but rivalry and hate.

"I can take care of myself, Enzo." She glanced my way for a beat then returned her attention to both her brothers. "Actually, I did need you a few days ago, but luckily, Rex was there to save me. He brought me here to protect me. The Society is under attack."

"And you believe that? You don't think this is all just to make himself look the hero?" Enzo advanced toward me, but Caterina cut him off.

"He's telling the truth. Someone came after Dad and me."

"Someone came after Mikey too. When we were in Atlanta." Massimo shrugged as if saying, "they're not lying."

But beyond that, he didn't bother to set Enzo straight, which meant they had come here with a plan. I stayed focused on my breathing, willing the pain in my shoulder away. Not much I could do about the ache in my heart.

"What do you want? I have a hard time believing you're here to check in on your little sister after all this time."

Pursing his lips, Enzo reached inside his suit jacket and retrieved a piece of paper. Caterina took it from him. From where I stood, all I could see was the emblem from the Crucible. It was a statement. If I had to guess, it was Michael's account statement from the Crucible.

Caterina crumbled the sheet in her hand and turned to me with glossy eyes. "Dad's debt."

I wanted to hold her and tell her it was all right. That her Dad didn't deserve all this pity and loyalty. "How did you get that?" I asked Enzo.

"We know why Caterina is here." Massimo cocked an eyebrow to emphasize his meaning.

The assholes thought I had paid for sex. I was okay with them thinking that. "I can't control your dad's actions. No more than you can." I stuffed my hands in my pockets to keep me from reaching out to Caterina. She seemed so alone and so hurt. "Get to the point."

"Did you tell Dad?" Caterina sucked in a breath. "Does he know?"

"Jesus, Caterina. Do you think he's an idiot? He told us. He sent us for you." After Enzo's stentorian revelation, the room fell eerily quiet.

"How did Dad find out?" She turned to me.

"Isn't it obvious?" I reached for her hand. "He sent you to me."

"Rex, you know I came to you of my own volition."

"That's not what I meant." This was the worst timing.

"What's done is done." Massimo stepped in. "His debt is settled."

"I don't believe you." A shock of adrenaline ran through me. Now I was afraid—afraid I was losing her.

"It's true." Caterina turned to face me. "The statement has been paid. How?"

"I had the money." Enzo shrugged. "When Dad explained, we came straight here."

Fuck my luck. From the moment Caterina signed our contract, I knew it would end sooner than I'd hoped it would. But I always assumed it would be after I had time to make her see we belonged together. After she had time to get to see that we weren't much different. That destiny had brought us together for a reason. The Society was still under attack. I needed her and I needed the Alfera family to back me up. What happened? Why did the old man change his mind about helping me?

"That's all fine. But Caterina and I still have a deal. Our agreement doesn't end until I say so." I stepped toward her, but both brothers stood at attention.

"You mean until the debt was paid." Caterina shot me a look of daggers.

"You read the contract. What did it say?"

She opened her mouth to speak. As the realization that we never discussed a way out of the contract by paying off Michael's debt, her eyes grew wider. The anger that registered there was enough to wipe the smirk off my face. It had a been a low blow to only put a timeline on the page, and not a form of payoff. But I never cared about the money. I cared about spending six months with her.

"You tricked me?" She finally snapped out of her bewilderment.

Well, it was more than that. She was, rightfully so, pissed off at me all over again. The million-dollar question was, would Caterina call my bluff? I was willing to push her to the limit, but I wasn't going to call the damn cops on her for refusing to honor a contract that was meant to serve as a conduit of trust more than a legal document.

"Seems we're at an impasse." I hit send on my phone. Before Caterina could think of any other insult, my guys barged in. "Caterina stays."

"Fuck off." Massimo fisted his hands. "Last night, I thought you wanted to help make a difference."

"I still do." Was I being the asshole? Absolutely. But Caterina would've stayed with me, if Enzo and Massimo hadn't come in here with their proverbial guns blazing, shaming her for what she did to save her dad. I met her gaze. She felt so far away. And to think that just minutes ago, she was in my arms calling for me. "Caterina, we don't need to be out of time. We belong together."

"You should've thought about that when you orchestrated this whole entrapment. I trusted you. I thought..."

"Enough." Enzo took the statement from her and stuffed it back in his coat. "We're going home right now. Get your things."

"I didn't bring anything with me." She scowled at me.

I bet they were both thinking the worst right about now. Fine. That one I did deserve. When she walked past me, I gripped her wrist. Her flowery scent was a shock to my senses. I had so much to say, but the right words didn't come to me. Instead, I thought of her tied up in my arms in complete surrender. "You're making a mistake."

"You lied."

"You know I don't do that." I pursed my lips.

"Oh no. I forgot. You bend the truth to suit you. Jesus, Rex. That's lying. I came here because of Dad. I think it's fitting that I leave here because of him, too." She yanked her arm away. "He needs me. They all do."

I need you. I wanted to say, but not here, not with her brothers watching us.

"Tell your men to step aside." Enzo wedged himself between me and Caterina.

I was taller than him and more than willing to fight back. But that would solve nothing. For the good of the Society, our families, I had to let her go. I had to forget about her and move on.

"Let them through," I said through gritted teeth.

Rage surged through me, hot and thick, until all I saw was red as both Enzo and Massimo escorted Caterina out the door. She crossed the threshold, and I held my breath, waiting for her to turn back and tell me she didn't want to go, to make her stay.

She made it all the way to the elevators before she turned to me with tears in her eyes. All that planning. In the end, I only managed to hurt her deeply.

"I'm sorry." I mouthed before the elevator's doors slid closed all the way.

CHAPTER 24
Epilogue

R<small>EX</small>

I slammed the front door and headed upstairs. My head swam, and all I could hear was the regret in Caterina's voice. Jesus Christ, I almost had her. She was in my arms and ready for me. Would it have made any difference for her if we'd had sex? Probably not. She had been so hurt and angry when she left. That was on me. I'd been so afraid to lose her. I lied to keep her and lost her anyway.

Halfway up the steps, my damn shoulder decided to act up and discharge a shock of pain down my back.

"Mother fucker." I leaned against the wall for support and slipped all the way to the floor. The cool marble brought some relief to my shoulder, which seemed to be bleeding again. Black spots hovered in front of my eyes and blocked my view of a pair of legs in high heels. "Caterina." I reached for her.

"For crying out loud. I knew this little experiment of yours wouldn't end well."

My eyes flew open and focused on Donata's face. I winced and glanced at my arm. "I think I passed out for a minute."

"You think? A chunk of your shoulder is trying to put itself back together. What part of stay in bed is so hard to understand?" She shook her head and hooked her arm around my waist to help me up. "Can you walk, or should I call your guys?"

"No. I can manage." I trudged to my suite and settled on the sofa facing the fireplace.

"You should lie down." Donata ambled to the side table and prepared a syringe, then sat next to me.

"I'm tired of the fucking bed." I waved her hand away. "No drugs. They make me stupid. Right now, I need to think."

I rested my head on the cushion and glared at the crown molding on the ceiling. What the hell had happened? In one fell swoop, I lost Caterina and the support of the Alfera family. No matter how hard I tried, I seemed to keep going backward instead of forward. I shot to my feet and strode to the bar cart to pour myself a whiskey.

"As your doctor, I'd like to point out that drinking in your condition is a bad idea." Donata strolled over to me and picked up a tumbler.

"As my doctor, are you going to stop me?" I filled her cup.

"Even as you are, I don't think I could." She clinked my glass. "Cheers."

She ushered me to the bed. I let her take off my shoes and fluff my pillows. When she was finished, she leaned her thigh on the side of the mattress, resting her drink against her chest. She studied me for a while, then finally spoke. "I heard everything."

"I'm sure you did. The Alfera brothers weren't exactly quiet."

"What do you see in her? I mean, sure, she's pretty. But she's afraid of her own shadow." She furrowed her brows.

Of course Donata would see Caterina's fear as a weakness. But the thing was, Caterina wasn't afraid for herself, she was afraid for her family. I valued that in her. Even if that was the very thing that separated us today.

"She cares about her family."

"I'm sure." She chuckled. "The old man must've done a number on her. What happens now, Rex? The old man seems to have changed his mind."

"It seems he has." I took a long swig of whiskey. "I believe he means to wage war on me to get his throne back."

"What a week you've had." She inhaled. "First you win the favor of the sweet princess. Then you get shot trying to help her brother. Then the other brother swoops in and rescues her." She pointed a long finger at me, looking up as if trying to remember all the fucked-up events of the past several days. "And now she hates you again. You should've married me when you had the chance."

"We would've killed each other in the first week." I barked out a laugh.

"For sure."

"As my doctor, shouldn't you be trying to make me feel better? Or at least give me some sound advice. I don't need a reminder of the shitshow my life has become."

She finished the rest of her whiskey and ambled back to the coffee table in the living area. When she returned, she had a syringe in her hand. "As your doctor, I recommend you take the goddamn meds and rest so you can heal."

"And as a friend?"

"Well." She offered me a one-shoulder shrug with a smug smile on her face. "As your friend, I suggest you take the fucking meds, rest so you can heal, and then give the old man a run for his money. He doesn't get to have his cake and eat it too."

"You're starting to sound like Vittoria."

"My aunt is a lot of terrible things. But she's rarely wrong." She sat next to me. "Rex, for once, my family and yours want the same thing. There's a cancer in the Society. We need to cut it out."

"Michael said the exact same thing." At the time, all I could think of was that Caterina could only be safe with me. I had my head so far up my ass, I didn't see through the old man's half-truths.

"You have my family's backing. But you know that in our world, friends are hard to come by. And even harder to keep." She braced her hands on her hips. "Desperate men will do and say anything."

"I know."

"Choose wisely, Rex."

I stared at the city lights beyond the tall windows. She was right. Donata understood this mafia world as well as me. She had her father's sister to teach her. I had Dad. Since I left Atlanta, two things didn't add up for me—one, how was Mikey Gallo able to escape two murder attempts in which his entire family ended up dead? Mikey wasn't that smart or lucky. And two, how was it that Michael, without proof, knew exactly who attacked him?

He was so quick to blame the FBI. And I fell for it. Michael knew I would know about Dad's history with the feds.

Yeah, they hated us, and we hated them right back. But wiping out an entire mafia family required resources and a shit-ton of knowledge. Secret information that only the board had.

Son of a bitch. Michael Alfera had gone too far this time.

"He's using her again. This time, he's using her to get to me." I fisted my hand in anger and my shoulder promptly protested. "She's an innocent. She doesn't deserve this."

"You want to live? Stay away from her. It's the only chance you have to win this fight with her father." Donata's eyes softened. She really wanted me to survive this. "You know I'm right."

"I do. But here's the thing. She was promised to me. She's mine."

"How did I know you were going to say that?" She puffed out a breath. "Michael thinks she makes you weak. Honestly, we all do."

"He wants ruthless. Fine."

I had failed today. Royally. But that didn't mean I was ready to give up on the promise I made to Dad. I swore to save the Society, reunite the families, and honor our code to protect our people. I wasn't about to give up just because some greedy, old man had decided he wanted to play king again.

This was far from over. I had been patient with Michael because of his long-standing friendship with Dad. But enough was enough. Fuck my luck. I knew what I had to do. And I was sure Caterina was going to hate me for it. For real this time.

I fished my phone out of the pocket of my sweats and called Frank. As usual he picked up on the first ring. I didn't wait for pleasantries. "Get my plane ready. We leave in the morning."

"You got it, boss. Where to?"

"Ibiza. Don't tell the onsite team we're coming."

"On it." Static filled the air, and I could tell he wanted to ask if Caterina was coming too.

"You and I are handling this alone. Make sure Caterina's security detail stays with her. I don't trust Michael."

"Yes, sir."

I hung up and glanced up at Donata, who had the biggest smile on her face.

"The king is back."

"I'm following your advice." I pointed at the syringe.

"What's in Ibiza?" She pumped me chockfull of pain killers, a cocktail of her own design.

"A hunch," I mumbled.

Up until now, I had been working under a shit-ton of assumptions and gut feelings. I needed proof now. I needed all the fucking names spelled out. For Caterina's sake, I hoped her father's wasn't on that list. The Society had very specific rules on this. And it forgave no one.

My mind slowly began to drift off, until the throbbing subsided. I closed my eyes and let the images of Caterina play in my head like a movie. At least I had that much. I had real memories of her. I knew how her skin smelled and what she tasted like. And that would have to be enough. Too many lives were at stake.

I couldn't afford to be weak. I had to let her go.

THANK you so much for reading King of Beasts, Book 1. I hope you enjoyed Caterina and Rex's wild ride. Rex and Caterina's epic love story concludes in King of Beasts (Beast Duet #2),

where Caterina learns the truth about Rex's plans and her father's contract with the Society.

Caterina Alfera, an angel lost in a world of beasts.
I didn't ask for her.
Destiny brought her to me.
And now I can't let her leave.
She's mine to keep.

Download King of Beasts (Beast Duet #2) today!

I've included the first chapter of King of Beasts (Beast Duet #2) so can you can try it for FREE. Go ahead, you know you want to. :-)

Do you want more Dark Mafia Romance? If you enjoy steamy reads, please do consider leaving a kind review. It lets me know you'd like to see more books like this one.

King of Beasts

DIANA A. HICKS

BEASTS DUET, BOOK #2

CHAPTER 1
Assholes with Guns

Rex

Caterina Alfera was safe at home. She stayed in her brother's apartment in the upper east side for the most part and only went to work twice a week, properly escorted. I re-read the daily account of Caterina's comings and goings until the letters blurred and ran into each other. Then I switched to the set of images of her.

I glared at the different stills of her eating lunch with a co-worker, shopping for flowers, getting a latte, and a bunch of other mundane things normal people did—as if the time we had spent together hadn't happened. A whole month had passed since I left New York City—since she left me. And I'd yet to figure out how to let her go. I shut the iPad screen and pushed it away.

Through the yacht window, the moonlight rays slanted across the oversize cabin. I imagined Caterina sitting on her heels in the pool of light on the floor. And fuck me if my entire body didn't ache to have her like that again. Caterina was my rope bottom for another five months. One way or another, I would get her to finish her contract with me. For now, I had to stay away from her.

For her own safety, I needed Michael to think he had won this round. Technically, he had. He took Caterina away from me, and I still had no clue who was killing Society members. The old man had covered his tracks well.

In all the weeks I had been in Ibiza, I didn't find anything that would indicate he was behind the assassination of the Gallo family. I also had no proof that the FBI was behind it all, or that he was the rat who sold us out. Because of him, the Society was about to be wiped out for good. I couldn't let that happen. I made a promise to Dad, and I intended to keep it.

"Permission to come aboard, Captain." Santino Buratti leaned on the door frame. His mussed hair and undone tie told me he had been out partying all night.

"Way to keep a low profile." I glanced at the clock on the mantel. It was three in the morning. Out of habit, I subtracted six hours to calculate the time in New York City. "You're here to help me find Mikey Gallo, not spend your nights drinking yourself stupid." I rose to my feet and walked around the desk.

The Buratti family was one of the five original families of the Society. An attempt on Santino's father's life made them realize that we were all in danger—that whoever killed the Gallos was coming for us next. When Santino found out I had traveled to follow a clue, he reached out to my guys and offered his help.

Together, we had been tracking Mikey's associates in Ibiza, but every bit of information so far had gotten us nowhere. I was beginning to think my gut had led me astray. I had been so sure that Mikey hadn't survived the attacks on his family because he was that lucky—that he was alive because he'd cut a deal. I had hoped someone in Ibiza would know who was behind it all. I needed a fucking name—or names. Because I was certain Michael wasn't acting alone.

"I'll have you know," he put up a finger and stumbled to a club chair, "I was out chasing a lead."

"And?"

"Another dead end." He shrugged and extended his legs out in front of him.

"I'm so tired of chasing smoke." I paced the length of the room, taking in the salty breeze wafting across the marina and the open windows below deck.

"I'm done with this bullshit trip too. It's time we go home, Rex." He shot a glance toward the door. "Which is why I did something you're not gonna like."

He waved a hand, and five guys barged in with their weapons pointed at my head. The son of a bitch sold me out. I glared at Santino. Blood pumped fast and hard through me while I considered my options. If I started shooting, I would get gunned down before I made it off the boat. *Fuck me.* My only way out was to get Santino to reconsider, to think about what his actions meant for the Society, and his family.

"We want the same thing, Santino. If I go down, we all go down. You just signed your own death warrant."

"Maybe." He perched his hip on the edge of the desk. "We've been trying to talk to these guys for weeks. They don't know anything. They're just assholes with guns."

"We have orders to bring him in." One of the men spoke up as he stepped toward me. By the tinge of fear in his eyes, I had to assume he knew exactly who I was.

"See? Now you get to meet their boss." He cocked his

eyebrow as if he were waiting for me to congratulate him for his brilliant plan.

"You served me up as bait."

"Caterina is messing with your ability to do your job, Rex. Don't pretend. We all know about you and her. Your relationship with her has gone beyond a business one. And not only that, but Michael Alfera has decided he no longer needs to uphold his end of the deal with your family."

I pursed my lips, wishing I could tell him he was wrong.

"You said you came here to get a name, find out who's after us. But I think you came here to prove Caterina's father is innocent in all this. When you know damn well that old man would sell his own flesh and blood to get what he wants. Because of Caterina, you're afraid to find out the truth, which is why all this time you haven't made a modicum of progress. You wanted the Buratti's family help? Here we are. Progress." He turned to the crew. "What the fuck are you waiting for? His permission? Take him."

In the next beat, all five men rushed me. I punched one of them square on the jaw, and then his gut. The effort didn't help my case. Without Santino's help, I had no shot at getting out. He stood back while the crew brought me down and let their leader put me in a chokehold. The last thing I saw before I blacked out was Mikey Gallo's face. *Son of a bitch.*

When I woke up, the sun was high up in the sky. Shimmering blue water sloshed against the yacht. In the distance, a sliver of land appeared. I squinted at it as I tried to catch my bearings. We were out to sea with not a single boat in sight. If Mikey wanted to kill me, this would be the perfect spot to do it. Easy clean up too since all he would have to do would be to shove me off the deck.

"You had it all. What did the FBI offer you that you didn't already have?" I scowled at Mikey.

Other than Michael Alfera's suppositions, I had no proof that the FBI was behind the killings, but Mikey didn't know that. Even if I didn't make it out of this one, I still wanted to know who betrayed us. Would Santino take that information back to his family and make things right? He'd always been somewhat of a lone wolf. I should've known he'd go off on his own to get answers.

"They offered me my life and freedom." He crossed his arms over his chest. "And a seat at the table. Something my own goddamned family never thought to offer me."

The circles under his eyes were more pronounced than they had been since I last saw him in Atlanta. That night I had gotten shot trying to help him. "The crew in Atlanta. They weren't after you, were they?"

"No. They were there for Massimo. But then you showed up."

"You betrayed your own best friend." I barked out a laugh. "Massimo spent days looking for you. He was worried about you. All the while, you didn't think twice to drag him all the way to Atlanta just to get him killed."

"I'm tired of living in the shadows. Living on the run. I love Massimo. But I love myself more. In the end, it all worked out. Massimo's still alive."

"You're a fucking coward. He could've been killed. How long do you think before the FBI decides they no longer need you? What do you think is going to happen then?"

"What do you care? You won't be here to see it." An older man strode on deck. The greasy hair and cheap suit were a dead giveaway. He was an agent.

"Who the fuck are you?" I met his gaze.

"I'm the hero. The one here to save the day." He glowered at me with so much hate and greed in his eyes, I could only assume he had been waiting for this day for a long time. The man had to be in his late sixties, which meant that at some point he had been chasing Dad too.

"Does our hero have a name?" I shifted my weight against the two men holding me down. The chair inched forward, and the pig shuffled back as if he were afraid of me—coward.

"Special Agent in Charge, Clifton." He offered me his hand, then chuckled. "I see you're tied up at the moment."

"Get on with it. What are you waiting for, Clifton?" I challenged him to make his move.

"I want to savor this moment. Michael didn't think I could do this. He thought you'd be harder to catch. Look at you. I'm not impressed." He pointed at the zip tie around my wrists.

"You didn't make a deal with Michael. What could you possibly offer Michael Alfera?"

"I have plenty to offer." He pointed a finger at me. "A new Society, for example."

Jesus Christ.

Made sense. I would bet the heads of all five Dons would earn Clifton a bunch of shiny medals within the bureau. With the board gone, Michael would have the opportunity to come in and build something new, completely under his command.

Where the hell was Santino? Did Clifton really let him go? Or was he dead? Santino was next in line to represent his family. He was already running most of the Buratti businesses. If Clifton was looking to catch big whales, Santino would be one of them—unless the asshole betrayed us too.

"I came to Ibiza to get a name." I slanted a glance behind

me and spotted two men next to Gallo. "And now I have three. I won't stop until you, Mikey, and Michael pay for what you did."

"Enough." Mikey strode into my line of sight. "Throw him overboard already. We're sitting ducks out here."

I peeked at the chopper headed our way, approaching fast. "Yes, you are."

The helicopter circled around us while bullets pelted relentlessly on the polished cockpit. In a matter of seconds, the yacht began to creak and slowly tilt. I stormed to my feet to take cover because the asshole shooting at us didn't seem to care who got hit. He continued to spray the boat with lead until I was the last one left on the foredeck with nowhere to go.

As soon as the machine gun stopped, fucking Santino lowered himself to the landing skid and threw me a fire escape rope ladder. Clifton and his men had disappeared. With the wreckage going under, I didn't have time to go look for them. Mikey had stayed behind, cowering by the closed door that led below deck. Clifton bailed on him.

I flipped over one of the men on the floor and took his weapon. "Fac Fortia et Patere." Do brave things and endure. I reminded Mikey of our mandate as members of the Society. "You betrayed your family," I yelled over the loud hum of the propellers, wincing against the strong wind and debris.

Mikey put up his hands and opened his mouth. I shot him before he had time to think of another lie to save his skin. The Society's by-laws were clear on this. Treason was punishable by death. I dropped the gun and released a breath.

"We don't have time for a memorial," Santino called over the loudspeaker.

Shit. I darted toward the chopper, but two steps in, the

deck gave out from under me. Fuck my luck. I inhaled and waited for the sea water to drag me under. When I resurfaced, I spotted Santino's rope ladder dangling a few feet away, and swam toward it.

"Hold on." He shouted a bunch of instructions I didn't quite hear over the loud screeching of the boat sinking several feet away.

Kicking hard with my legs, I hooked my elbows around the top step and let Santino and his men pull me up. As soon as I landed inside the cockpit, we veered away from the wreckage.

"You fucking asshole!" I shot to my feet and shoved him onto the seat. "I could've been killed."

"I told you, you were not gonna like my plan." He sat back on his captain chair with a wolfish grin on his face. "Did you get us a name?"

"I did."

"I may not agree with you on a lot of things, Rex. But we're family. Whether we like it or not. We stick together. Mikey Gallo forgot that. And now he's dead."

"Yeah." I nodded while he cut the zip tie around my wrists. "And Clifton?"

"I have a cleanup crew on their way to scour what's left of the yacht. We'll know soon. You got a name?" He cocked his head to look me in the eye. "I gotta hear you say it."

"Michael Alfera," I confirmed the name for him.

Michael Alfera, Caterina's dad, was working with the FBI to wipe us all out. Of course, I had to assume that, at some point, the old man was thinking about betraying the FBI too. It was obvious to me that the only reason he aligned himself with someone like Clifton was because he wanted to come out of retirement and be king again. Except, that position was already taken—I was the king.

"Alfera betrayed us. The by-laws are clear on this, Rex."

"Yes, they are. Michael will answer for what he did. I'll make sure of that."

"You're thinking about his daughter? Jesus, fuck!" He threw his hands up in frustration. "This is why marriages within the families are forbidden."

"More like frowned upon."

"Your dad made a mistake agreeing to Alfera's deal. And now, here we are dealing with the consequences of his actions. But here's the thing, I don't give a shit about what Caterina wants. She'll have to get on board. As for you, you need to stop thinking with your dick and start acting like a king." He winced and swallowed hard.

"I recognize that look on your face." I pointed at his side. "You got hit."

Jesus Christ, Clifton's men were so busy shooting at the chopper, they didn't think to kill me. Santino had taken a huge risk using us both as bait. A risk that had paid off. So, I couldn't be all that pissed off at him, especially since he had been right in his assumptions. A part of me had hoped to find evidence that Caterina's dad wasn't involved with the FBI.

"It's just a scratch." He winced.

I chuckled thinking of how mangled my shoulder had been the last time a bullet grazed me. The wound had taken weeks to heal, mostly because the muscle was shredded in different spots. I tapped the pilot on the shoulder. "How close can you get us to the hospital?"

"Absolutely not," Santino blurted out.

"I have an arrangement with the local doctor. She'll patch

you up." I helped him out of his suit jacket. Sure enough, the sleeve of his dress shirt was soaked in blood. "You'll have to wait until we're back in New York to get one of Donata's reviving cocktails."

"You're stalling." He met my gaze. "If you fail to deliver on this, the other families will find a way to unseat you."

"I'm well aware of what's at stake here. And I know what I have to do."

Within the Society, treason was punishable by death. Michael Alfera had crossed the line when he cut a deal with a pig. If left unchecked, he would continue to murder key members of the board, starting with me, Signora Vittoria, and Santino's dad. I had to order Michael's execution.

But Santino was right. I was thinking about Caterina and how losing more family would kill her. I was thinking about how much she would hate me for doing my job. I was thinking about how if I went through with it, she would never love me.

But what choice did I have?

———

Rex and Caterina's epic love story concludes in
King of Beasts (Beast Duet #2)

Made in United States
North Haven, CT
25 May 2023

36984509R00150